JUNGLE RULES

A NOVEL OF VIET NAM

By

Gaz Crittenden

Fiction // ISBN 0-89754-219-3
$16.95

gazcrittenden@comcast.net

Cover design by Chris Genter and Sheila Gallagher
Cover photo by Abby Pope

Dan River Press
PO Box 298
Thomaston, ME 04861

In memory of

Jim Schueller

and

John Tarantowicz

Two who did not make it back.

Contents:

I.   WAKE-UP IN NAM

Alive. Fingers, hands, arms, trunk, testicles, legs, feet, toes: *All present and accounted for.* He opens his eyes. A faint gray light is glowing in the eastern sky. Another day in the Nam.

Rolling out of his poncho, he rises creakily and unbuttons his trousers. His urine splashes and steams in the early morning air. Sitting down again, he takes off his boots and socks and carefully checks his feet, rubbing antifungal powder between the toes and applying Bacitracin ointment to the cracks in the soles. Next he takes his extra pair of socks out from under his shirt. They have spent the night next to his skin, and his body heat has dried them out completely. The wool-polyester blend feels luxurious as he slips his feet into them, then pulls his boots back on, re-laces and ties them.

Inspecting his web gear, he finds that a scorpion has spent the night curled up next to one of his ammo pouches. He shakes it off, watches it as it scuttles away. *Good luck, little fella. Have a nice day.*

With his sheath knife he scrapes a hole in the ground and cuts a small chunk off the brick of C-4 plastic explosive that he carries with him for making fires. After pouring a measure of water from his canteen into the metal cup, he places the C-4 in the hole and lights a corner of it with his Zippo. Quickly he places the cup over the hole, as a superhot yellow flame leaps high. Within seconds, the water is boiling. He dumps in packets of C-ration coffee and cocoa and stirs them with a plastic spoon. He takes a sip of the piping hot drink. *A-a-a-h-h!* The potent mixture delivers a jolt to his brain as efficiently as if he had

1

injected it into a vein.

His head throbs painfully, a hangover from chronic dehydration. As he will not have a chance to refill his canteen until they find a village well, he takes an APC along with the malaria pills that he washes down with the mocha coffee. With the P-38 can opener that he wears on his dogtag chain he opens a can of peaches. He eats the fruit slowly with the plastic spoon, chewing each mouthful many times, savoring every bite. When he has consumed all the peaches, he licks every last bit of syrup residue from the spoon and can.

With some bumwad and an entrenching tool, he heads for the perimeter. Choosing a likely spot, he drops his trousers and hunkers down. Like most of the grunts, he wears no underwear, as it chafes and causes rashes. The air feels cool on the bare skin of his ass. From a nearby foxhole, a voice calls:

"Hey, Target, hope everything comes out all right!"

From the other side:

"Take one for me, Targ!"

He feels not the slightest embarrassment. When he first arrived here, it bothered him to have to perform his bodily functions in front of others. Now he shits as naturally as an animal, or a Vietnamese. Like the peaches, like the coffee, a good shit is one of the pleasures of his morning, and he enjoys it immensely. Finishing his business, he sits down with his back against a tree and watches the sun rise out of the South China Sea.

The monsoon is beginning to break, and there are patches of blue amid the towering heaps of cumulus. The sun's rays illuminate the valley below him, lighting it up in a thousand shades of green. A river snakes through the valley, its brown serpentine curves widening as they approach the sea. He sees the hill that they are to climb this morning, and at its base a village, a collection of thatched huts nestled on the bank of the river beneath sheltering palms. His flared nostrils pick up a hint of pungent wood smoke. He can smell the motherfuckers.

Anger sends a rush of adrenaline coursing through his veins: anger at Charlie for killing his comrades; anger at the Vietnamese people for their apathy, antipathy and ingratitude; anger at his country for its failure of support; anger at himself for... what? Cowardice? Stupidity? Loss of honor, faith and patriotism? The anger is always there, simmering below the surface, and he feeds on it. It is what drives him, what keeps him going, what holds the fear at bay.

2

Standing up, he field strips the butt of his cigarette, letting the shreds of paper and tobacco drift to the ground and crushing out the glowing ash with his boot. It is time to get back to business.

"Rise and shine, ladies, it's a beautiful day for killing the babies!"

II.   LAST NIGHT IN THE WORLD

One of the things you learned in the course of your Army training was how to fall asleep at the drop of a hat. Andrew Cullen was unaware of the farmland of upper New York State gliding past the window. He had closed his eyes when the train left Grand Central Station, and, except for a brief period of wakefulness during the stop in Albany, had been bagging z's for the entire five-hour trip. He dreamed that he was marching, his limbs twitching with the cadence sung by the wheels on the track.

You also learned to stay alert, even in slumber. At the conductor's call that they were approaching the Utica station, he came instantly awake. He tightened the knot of his necktie, buttoned his green uniform jacket and placed his overseas cap squarely on his head. Rising, he retrieved his AWOL bag from the overhead rack and walked down the aisle toward the end of the coach, easily adjusting his balance to the train's swaying motion. The train slowed, gliding into the station, and after a long, metallic squeal of brakes, bumped gently to a halt. Andy Cullen had come home.

Stepping off the train with a handful of other passengers, and finding the platform empty, he proceeded up the stairs to the main terminal. The vast waiting room, with its marble columns and high coffered ceilings, recalled Utica's heyday, when it had been a major textile center and one of the fastest growing cities in the state. There were his family, standing near the newspaper kiosk: his father, bald

5

and barrel-chested, with the naturally scowling expression that Andy had inherited to a lesser degree; his mother, careworn but still lovely, in a faded dress long out of fashion; and his little sister, pug-nosed and freckled, a miniature version of himself, and a foot taller than he remembered her. Lucy was the first to catch sight of him and came racing towards him like a whirlwind, all knobby knees and elbows and red pigtails flying. She nearly bowled him over as she leapt on him and clung to him tightly.

"Hello, Goosey Lucy," he said, hugging her back, his vocal cords strangely thick.

His parents sidled up to them, and he gently disengaged himself from his sister's embrace.

"You look thin," his mother remarked as he kissed her cheek. Have they been feeding you enough?"

"He looks lean and mean," his father corrected her. "He looks pretty good, really, for a dogface."

His father had been a Navy Seabee in the "Big One." The "dog-face" remark was an attempt at manly inter-service teasing, and was as close to humor as his father ever got.

"How long will you be staying?" his mother asked.

"Just for tonight, Mom. I have to be back at Fort Jackson by five o'clock tomorrow afternoon."

"You came all this way," his father asked incredulously, "just to turn around and go right back again?"

"That's right, Pop. I wanted to see you guys before I ship out."

"You're shipping out? Where are you going?"

"I'm not supposed to say, Pop. You know the drill."

"Well, if this visit is costing five bucks a minute, we better get going. Come on, we're parked out front."

The blue '59 Impala sedan was as pristine and spotless as ever and glowed under a fresh coat of wax. After throwing his AWOL bag in the trunk, Andy climbed into the back seat with Lucy. On the ride home, there was little conversation. His father tuned the radio to an International League baseball game in which the Syracuse Chiefs were playing the Toledo Mud Hens. Next to him, Lucy squirmed and fidgeted, dying to chatter, but knowing that to do so would bring down their father's wrath. Finally her impatience got the better of her, and she asked about the red and yellow ribbon on his chest.

"What's that, Andy? Did they give you a medal?"

"Quiet back there!" Angus Cullen snapped. "Mack Jones is up."

6

"It's the National Defense Service Medal," Andy whispered. "Every active duty soldier gets one."

They turned off the paved road onto the long dirt driveway leading to the family's cedar-shingled bungalow. His father pulled the car into the garage (no unnecessary exposure to the elements for this baby), and after Andy retrieved his bag from the trunk, they all trooped up the porch steps. Opening the front door, he was almost knocked down a second time, as the family's Labrador Retriever crashed into him full tilt. He knelt and put his arms around the dog, burying his fingers in the thick fur.

"Raven, did you miss me, boy? I missed you too!"

The dog responded by licking his face and making little whining sounds.

"You must have missed lunch," his mother said. "Let me fix you something to eat."

"No thanks, Mom, I had a sandwich on the train. Actually, I'm kind of tired. I think I'll just go and lie down for awhile."

"Actually," his father mimicked, "I was thinking you might want to mow the lawn. It hasn't been getting much attention since you left."

His face must have betrayed his horror, for his father laughed and clapped him on the back.

"Just kidding, sport. Go ahead and take it easy. You've earned it."

After all these years, the old man could still get his goat. Andy retreated down the hall and entered his room, closing the door behind him. It was like stepping through a time warp. Everything was exactly as he remembered it: the Jap rifle that his father had brought back from the Pacific as a souvenir; the collection of basketball trophies on the bureau; the Syracuse pennant on the wall (his boyhood dream had been to play hoops for the Orangemen). Even the musty smell in the air was familiar and comforting. He kicked off his spit-shined low-quarter shoes, removed his blouse and stretched out on the bed.

His old bed was considerably larger than his Army bunk, and infinitely more comfortable. Lying on his back with his hands clasped behind his head, he watched dust motes drifting in a shaft of sunlight coming through the window. For the first time in almost a year, he felt that he could let his guard down, that he was completely safe. It was almost like returning to the womb.

He did not know why he started crying. One moment he was

feeling perfectly content, and in the next, his chest heaved with wracking sobs. Rolling over, he buried his face in the pillow to stifle the sounds that he was making. He had not wept this way since he was a child. What was happening to him?

There was a knock at the door, and his sister's voice called softly: "Andy? Andy?"

He lay still, pretending to be asleep. It would not do for her to see him this way.

"Come on, big brother, I know you're in there. You aren't doing anything bad in there, are you? Don't bother looking for those Playboys you hid under your mattress. Mom found them and took them away."

That got his attention. Leaping off the bed, he lifted the mattress. His Playboy collection was still intact. He could hear the little imp giggling as she ran away down the hall. He wondered if she knew about their father's stash of skin magazines in the garage. He decided that she probably did- she had her nose into pretty much everything. He lay down again, chuckling, and closed his eyes. A little sleep was all he needed. A little sleep, and he would be fine.

*

When he opened his eyes, it was still light outside his window. His watch said it was after seven-thirty. He got up and padded down the hall to the kitchen in his stocking feet. His mother and sister were there, cleaning up the supper dishes.

"We decided to let you sleep," his mother told him, "but I saved you some pot roast. Sit down at the kitchen table, and I'll bring you some."

"That's okay, Mom, I don't think I want any right now. I'll probably be going out."

"But pot roast is your favorite!"

"I'll have some later, when I get home."

"Well, then, maybe you'd like a little something to tide you over."

She reached into a paper bag, and took out a cellophane-wrapped package which she handed to him.

"Devil Dogs! Oh, Mom, you're the greatest!"

He tore the wrapping off the package and opened the fridge,

taking out a carton of milk. Cramming one of the chocolate snack cakes into his mouth, he took a big swig from the carton. Delicious! His mother opened her mouth as if to say something, then closed it again. Andy took the wall phone off the hook and dialed a number from memory.

"Hello, Swino? It's Andy... Yeah, it's me! How ya doing, man? I'm home on leave, and I was wondering what you're doing... Yeah, I've finished my training, I'm a trained killer now... A party? Cool! Are you still in the same house?... Cool! I'll see you in a few minutes."

"I'm going over to Billy Swinford's, Mom," he said, hanging up the phone. "Where's Pop? I need to borrow the car."

"Can I come with you?" Lucy asked.

"Sure, kid. In about eight more years."

He found his father in the family room, drinking Scotch whiskey and watching "Gunsmoke" on television. The old man busted his chops, treating him like a teenager and making him promise to be home by midnight, but that was no surprise, and Andy was soon heading out the door, whistling, with the car keys in his hand.

Billy Swinford lived off-campus in a seedy neighborhood bordering on the Erie Canal. As he parked the car a block from the house, Andy could hear shouts and laughter, and the blaring trumpets of Herb Alpert and the Tijuana Brass. The front door was open wide, and he walked into the midst of a party in full swing. The living room was packed with young people wearing jeans and shorts and miniskirts, all shouting to make themselves heard above the din. He did not see anyone he recognized, so he pushed on through the crowd, looking for Swino.

"Holy shit, Cullen, is that you?"

In baggy cutoff jeans and a Hawaiian shirt, Billy Swinford looked like a troll dressed up as a human. At six-five, he was short for a center, but what he lacked in height he more than made up for in ferocity. His rubbery features were contorted in disbelief as he gaped at his former teammate. Andy suddenly felt self-conscious in his uniform. Funny, it had not even occurred to him to change into civilian clothes.

"Yeah, Swino, it's me. Do I really look that different?"

"Fuckin' A, man, you look like a fuckin' Nazi or somethin'. I'll say one thing for you, though, you look like you're in shape. You look like you could go ten rounds with Muhammad Ali."

"Like I told you, I'm a trained killer."

"Hey, it's really great to see you, man. Help yourself to anything

9

you want. I'll catch you later, okay?"

The crowd parted for Billy as if by magic, and closed behind him, swallowing him up. Andy felt disappointed. He had expected Swino to fill him in on what had been going on while he was away.

On the porch off the kitchen he found a tub of iced Genesee Cream Ale. He drank one straight down, then popped open another and returned to the party, where the crowd was rocking to the Kingsmen's unintelligible rendition of *Louie Louie.* He remained on the fringes of the gathering, watching the dancers with amusement, returning frequently to the tub of Genny Cream. He felt older than these kids, and wiser. He decided it was time to leave Swino's party. The evening was short, and he had another stop to make.

"Hey there, soldier."

The speaker was a petite, curly-headed girl wearing tight jeans and a halter top that left her midriff bare. She was a bit on the plump side, but her face was very pretty, ivory-complected, with liquid brown eyes.

"You probably don't remember me," she continued. "I'm Andrea Santorelli. I was a year behind you at Proctor High, and I was on the cheerleading squad. I was one of your biggest fans."

"Sure I remember you," he lied. "So, Andrea, do you go to Mohawk Community now?"

"That's right, and I'm still a basketball junkie. I know all the guys on the team. Swino is my favorite. He throws the greatest parties! I heard you were on the freshman team last year, Andy. But you left school, hunh, joined the Army?"

"Yeah, there's this thing going on over in Viet Nam, you know? I thought I'd check it out."

"Wow, that's amazing! Are you a Green Beret or something?"

"No, I'm just what you might call an ordinary dogface."

"Isn't it, you know, kind of dangerous?"

"I guess so, maybe. But it will take more than a bunch of commie rice farmers to stand up to the American Army."

"Wow, you're really brave. And you look so handsome in that uniform. Hey, you wanna dance?"

The stereo was playing a slow number by The Righteous Brothers. It was plain that she was coming on to him, and Andy was tempted. But he was a man on a mission.

"Sorry, Andrea, I was just leaving. It's my last night at home, and there's someone I've got to see."

"She's a lucky girl. Keep safe, Andy."

Andrea stood on tiptoe and kissed him. Her lips were soft and plush, and he was surprised by a dizzying rush of sensation that momentarily buckled his knees. It occurred to him that he was making a big mistake, but he stuck to his guns. He turned his back on her and walked away.

*

He found another party in progress at the Munsons', but this was an entirely different world from the one he had just left. The lights of the big house were all aglow, and an orchestra was playing "Begin the Beguine." A uniformed policeman waved a flashlight, directing him to park in the field below the barn. Navigating carefully over the bumpy ground, he passed several rows of cars before managing to find a place. With the stiff gait of someone trying to hide the amount he had been drinking, he walked past the cop and up the gravel driveway to the front steps.

"Why, Mr. Cullen, we haven't seen you in the longest time!"

Effie, the Munson's colored maid, took his cap and greeted him warmly as he came inside. Before her retirement, she had been "Miss Hamblin," a teacher in the grade school that Andy had attended as a boy. It bothered him to see her working as a servant, and it made him uncomfortable to have her call him "Mister." But he supposed that the nature of Effie's employment was her own business.

The Munsons were the only people he knew with a room large enough to be legitimately called a ballroom. The dance floor was crowded with couples, mainly of the older generation. The women were dressed in evening gowns, while the men wore Madras jackets with trousers in ridiculous pastel colors. As he approached the bar that had been set up on a linen-covered table, the red-jacketed bartender cocked an inquiring eyebrow.

"Can I help you, sir?"

There would be no Genny Cream here. He ordered a gin and tonic and sipped it as he scanned the room, looking for Joan. The band was attempting a sanitized version of "The Twist." He spotted Joan's younger sister, Ruthie, gyrating wildly to the music. Her partner, a pimply-faced boy whose head barely reached her chin, was struggling vainly to keep up with her. His clumsy, uncoordinated movements evoked in Andy feelings of sympathy. He had been there.

Goddamn, but these drinks were small. They barely seemed to last two minutes. Making his way back to the bar, he bumped into a stout, red-faced man who glared at him in outraged surprise. The look that Andy gave him back caused the man's squinty eyes to slide down and away.

That's right, buddy. You don't mess with a trained killer.

It was then that he saw her, standing alone near the bar as if she had been waiting for him there all evening. As always, he was unprepared for the jolt that he experienced at the sight of Joan Munson. Her tawny mane of hair fell in a tangle over her shoulders. The simple white muslin dress that she wore and the strand of pearls at her throat contrasted with her deep suntan. The skin had peeled at the tip of her nose, leaving a spot the color of raspberry sherbet. Her chin was raised in profile, a smile tugging at the corners of her mouth, as she watched the dancers.

"Buy you a drink, gorgeous?"

As she turned to look at him, her electric blue eyes widened in recognition.

"My God, Andy! Where did you come from?"

"South Carolina, actually. Sorry to crash your party, Joan. I'm going away for awhile, and I wanted to say goodbye."

"Don't be silly. If I'd known you were going to be around, I would have invited you. Gosh, it's great to see you. You look so handsome in that uniform."

First Andrea, and now Joan. Could there actually be some truth to what they said about the attractiveness of men in uniform? Andy felt his ears burning. Sticking out from his head like jug handles, they proclaimed his embarrassment like neon signs.

"What are you drinking, Joan?"

"Someone's already getting me something. Ah, here he comes now. John, I'd like you to meet Andy Cullen. Andy, this is John Palmer."

The tall, bespectacled fellow looked like a geek, but the wrists protruding from his ill-fitting dinner jacket were sinewy, and his hands held a pair of highball glasses as if they were thimbles.

"Oops," he said, transferring a glass to his left hand in order to shake Andy's with his right, "spilled a little there, I'm afraid."

"John is a rower," Joan said, getting the credentials established, "the bow man on the Cornell crew. Andy is an old, old friend. Would

12

you mind giving us a few minutes, John-o? We have some catching up to do."

"Of course, sweetheart." John Palmer bent to kiss Joan's cheek, as he handed her a drink. "Nice meeting you, Andy."

"'Sweetheart,'" Andy repeated, when the tall fellow was out of earshot. "Sounds pretty serious."

"Oh, I suppose so," Joan replied, with a toss of her hair, "but there are still others in the running. What about you, Andy, do you have a girl?"

"I'm still holding out for you, Joanie."

"Oh, Andrew," she gasped, clutching her heart, "if I could only believe it were true!"

They always joked like this, even though they both knew that she was way out of his league. The problem was, in his case it was no joke. He had been in love with Joan since he was twelve.

"Come on," she said, taking his hand, "let's go outside where we can talk in private."

Torches were burning along the railing that enclosed the flag-stone terrace. Below them, a meadow swept down and away from the rear of the house before rising again toward the foothills of the Adirondacks. The sky was streaked with the last remnants of a spectacular sunset.

"So," he asked her, "how do you like Skidmore?"

"To tell you the truth, it's an awful bore. All those women! How do you like the Army?"

"It's really boring- you know, all those guys."

"Come on, Andy, tell me what it's really like."

"It's tough physically, but for someone who's played sports like me it's not really all that hard. Actually, I'm pretty good at it. The hardest part is we never get enough sleep. The drill sergeants yell at us all the time, but everyone knows it's just an act. It's like we're all playing a game together, acting out our parts. Sometimes it seems kind of silly, but there is a purpose to it, I think. We're learning to do what we're told, no matter how stupid it seems."

"What are the other guys like?"

"They're great! One of the best things about the Army is that it brings together all kinds of people. My best friend is a colored guy named Clarence Tyree. Ty is from Mississippi, and he says he never owned a pair of shoes before he joined the Army. A lot of the guys think that's a joke, but I'm not so sure. Ty is big and strong as an ox,

13

but he's just a nice quiet guy, and absolutely nothing fazes him. Growing up around here, I hardly knew any colored people, and I sure didn't have any as friends."

"Effie is the only colored person I know well. She is like a member of our family."

"Ty is like a brother to me. We're both Eleven Bravos, which is the Military Occupation Specialty, or 'MOS,' for infantryman. We're going to the same unit, so I hope we can stay together when we're over there."

"'Over there?' Andy, you're not going to Viet Nam, are you?"

"That's where I'm going, all right."

"But everyone is saying… oh, God, Andy, I can't believe this… you're so young… God, I need a cigarette. Have you got one?"

Andy produced a pack of Marlboros, shook one loose for her and pulled out his Zippo. He had been practicing popping it open with his thumb and forefinger, a slick move requiring more dexterity than he possessed in his present state of inebriation. The lighter flew from his hand and clattered on the flagstones, sliding beneath the railing.

It was necessary for him to get down on his hands and knees to retrieve it. As his fingers closed about the polished steel, he found himself gazing from a distance of six inches at Joan's foot, daintily encased in a white satin high-heeled shoe. It seemed at that moment the most exquisite thing he had ever seen. On an impulse, he pressed his lips to the instep and kissed it. Her voice came to him from far away.

"What do you think you're doing?"

He did not have the faintest idea. He had never done anything like this before, but he decided that he might as well be hanged for a sheep as for a goat. He continued kissing his way up over her smooth-muscled calf. Shocked by his own boldness, he was sure that at any moment Joan would tell him to stop; yet she did not. She leaned back against the railing, and it even seemed that she shifted her feet slightly to give him better access. Beneath the flimsy shelter of her dress, he breathed in the fragrances of cocoa butter and perfume, with a hint of something else mixed in, an animal scent that aroused his most primitive senses.

"Oh, God, someone's coming!"

Fireworks exploded before his eyes, as she jumped away from him, and her knee crashed into his nose. The pain was excruciating. He sat back on the flagstones, holding his hands to his face. Kneeling beside him, Joan was giggling hysterically.

"Oh, Andy- tee-hee!- I'm so sorry- tee-hee!- Are you all right-tee-he-he-he-heeeee?"

"I'm fine," he replied with annoyance, as he gingerly probed the bridge of his nose with his fingertips. As far as he could tell, it was not broken, and he did not feel any blood.

"What seems to be the trouble here?"

A tall, gray-haired gentleman was gazing down at them with concern. Joan could only splutter as she tried to suppress her giggles, so it was up to Andy to respond.

"No problem, sir. I tripped and bumped my nose on the railing. We're fine, everything's fine."

The man strolled on, muttering something about the ability of young people to hold their liquor. Andy and Joan clambered to their feet. She retrieved her cigarette, and he lit it for her. Her face was flushed in the glare of the lighter.

"My goodness," she said, breathing out smoke, "you've certainly learned a thing or two."

Although her impression of him was mistaken, it made him feel absurdly proud.

"I'm sorry, Joanie. I don't know what came over me."

"That's all right. It was... interesting."

She tossed the cigarette over the railing, where it sparked and went out on the grass.

"I should go back inside. John will be wondering what has become of me."

"I'll say goodbye, then. Take care, Joan. Wherever I am, I'll always be thinking about you."

She hugged him hard, and her cheek, pressed against his, was wet with tears.

"I love you, Andy. You're my very best friend. Let me know where you are, and I'll write to you."

Her heels clicked on the flagstones, as she hurried back towards the ballroom. Andy watched her until she disappeared inside, then walked around the side of the house to the driveway. The field with its gleaming rows of parked cars stretched below him. He had no trouble finding the Impala, which stood out like a poor and uncouth relation among the Caddys and Mercedes and Lincoln Continentals. In the distance, he could hear the orchestra playing *Just One of Those Things*.

He had done what he had come home to do. He had said his goodbyes. When you came right down to it, there was not very much for him in Utica anymore. He felt disconnected, disembodied, almost as if he had become a ghost. He turned the key in the ignition, and the Impala's engine rumbled to life. He would be home well before midnight; his father would be pleased.

III.   WAR BIRD

In the belly of the silver bird the air was cold. The men strapped eight abreast in the rear-facing seats sprawled in postures of exhaustion, mouths gaping, arms dangling limp. No longer did their faces bear the taught expressions evident when they boarded the aircraft. Seventeen hours in the air had rendered them nearly comatose.

Amid the rows of reclining figures, one young man was awake. PFC Andrew Cullen tried to read the Harold Robbins paperback that he had purchased during their refueling stop in the Philippines, but was too keyed up to concentrate. The words were a meaningless jumble on the page.

He saw himself in terms of the movies he had loved as a boy. One of his all-time favorites was *She Wore a Yellow Ribbon,* starring John Wayne. He did not actually remember much of the movie's plot, having been very young when he saw it; but he recalled very clearly how dashing the cavalrymen had looked in their blue uniforms with the gold stripe down the trousers. Fate had now decreed that he was to be a cavalryman himself. Not on horseback, of course. The Air Cav rode helicopters like sky chariots into battle. But they were the same units that used to ride horses, and their traditions dated back to the days of George Armstrong Custer. Amid the whine of the jet transport's engines, he could almost hear the strains of the old cavalrymen's tune, *GarryOwen.*

Intellectually, of course, he understood that this was not a movie. That he could actually die in Viet Nam had occurred to him. Aside from movie portrayals, however, his own experience of death was limited. He once had killed a songbird with his BB gun (and had

17

felt such remorse that the weapon had rested at the back of his closet ever since). He had gazed down at his grandmother lying in her casket. And he had lost a classmate in the random lottery of car crashes that culled a small percentage of every generation of American teenage boys. He was used to perceiving the risk of death as so remote as to be, essentially, irrelevant. It had not yet sunk in that he is now entering a very different lottery, one in which his own life was the prize.

There was little that Andy knew about the war to which he and his comrades were speeding, except that it was being fought to defend a country against communist aggression. When he graduated from high school, he had never even heard of Viet Nam. America's leaders had determined that the place was worth fighting for, and that was good enough for him.

Unlike commercial airliners, the C-141 Starlifter had no windows in the cabin. Andy got up and made his way down the aisle toward the tail of the aircraft, where there were two small portholes near the exit doors. Reaching the back row of seats, the only ones that faced forward, he crossed to a window and pressed his nose to the thick glass. There was nothing to be seen outside but a dizzying expanse of blue so bright it hurt to look at it, and so vast it was hard to tell where the sky ended and the sea began. A sudden attack of vertigo caused him to stagger backward. He tripped over an outstretched leg and stepped down hard on the toe of a spit-shined shoe.

His blunder was greeted by a surprised and angry cry. Recovering his balance, he stared into the flushed and contorted face of a man at least twice his age, who wore the stripes of a first sergeant on his sleeve.

"Geez," he blurted, "I'm sorry!"

"Sorry?" The first sergeant's mouth worked, as he tried to find the words to express his outrage. "You're goddamn right you're sorry! A sorry excuse for a soldier is what you are! Look what you've done to my shoe, you fuckin' shitbird!"

Roused by the commotion, the men in the neighboring seats looked on with interest. Although far from unusual in the military experience, the spectacle of a senior NCO dressing down a private offered a welcome diversion from the boredom of the flight. Andy knew better than to open his mouth again. To his relief, the older man's eyes softened as they read the black plastic nametag on his chest.

"'Cullen.' What outfit are you going to, Private Cullen?"

"First Air Cav, first sergeant."

18

"Eleven Bravo?"

"That's right, first sergeant."

"I'm a Cav replacement too. Won't be needing low quarters where we're going, will we, Cullen?"

"I guess not, first sergeant."

"Good luck, son. Keep your head down."

Andy felt his ears burning as he hurried back to his seat. He considered himself fortunate to have gotten off so lightly. The first sergeant had actually proven to be a pretty nice guy. If this had been a movie, their paths would have crossed again in some jungle hellhole, where he would have found the sergeant gravely wounded and carried him to safety through a hail of bullets. Given that the man looked as if he weighed a good two hundred and fifty pounds, they would have had to use his stunt double.

A crackling of the public address system drew attention to the Air Force tech sergeant who was standing in the aisle with a microphone in his hand.

"Gentlemen," he announced, "we are approaching the coast of Viet Nam, and in about fifteen minutes we will be arriving at Pleiku. Please observe the no smoking and seat belt signs when they are turned on. When we have landed, remain in your seats until you receive further instructions from Army personnel who will meet us on the ground. You may be interested to know that the weather in Pleiku is rainy, the temperature is 85 degrees."

The pop of the microphone being switched off was a signal that transformed the tranquil scene in the cabin to one of feverish activity. The few soldiers who were still asleep were jolted awake by the elbows of their neighbors. A drone of excited conversation overrode the sound of the engines, as men bent to tie their shoes and secure their hand luggage.

In the seat next to Andy, PFC Clarence Tyree stretched his long-muscled arms and yawned hugely.

"Hey, man," he said, "are we dere already?"

Andy repeated what the Air Force crew chief had said. Ty took a crumpled pack of Luckies from his breast pocket, shook one loose and offered the pack to Andy.

"Dat a fact?" he said, lighting both cigarettes with his Zippo. "Seem lahk we jus' lef' Travis."

To Andy, for whom every minute of the flight had been an agony of anticipation, Ty's casual attitude was astounding.

19

"Tell me something," he asked, "is there anything at all that gets you excited?"

Ty thought about that, blowing a long plume of smoke at the ceiling.

"Nope," he decided.

The signs flashed on: NO SMOKING; FASTEN SEAT BELTS. The young men barely had time to stub out their cigarettes before the plane pitched forward and went into a screaming dive. This was merely a standard tactic used by the pilots to avoid ground fire, but the passengers had no way of knowing this. They gripped the armrests of their seats with white-knuckled hands, certain that they were about to die. The plane leveled off sharply, crushing them into their seats, and then there came a sickening moment of weightlessness before the wheels touched down with a squeal and a jolt on the runway. The engines roared, applying reverse thrust, and they jerked to an abrupt stop. A collective sigh filled the cabin.

Ty raised a limp hand.

"No mo', boss, no mo'. Ah'll be good."

The door of the aircraft slid open, and a tanned Army sergeant dressed in jungle fatigues stepped into the center of the aisle. Picking up the crew chief's microphone, he called for attention.

"Men," he announced, "welcome to the Republic of Vet Nahm. You are now in a combat zone. When you unload the aircraft, do exactly as I say and do it smartly. Charlie has been known to pot at planes here on the runway with mortars, and your pilot would like to get moving along. All right, the crew are opening the doors now. When I give the word, I want you to move in an orderly fashion out the front and rear exits and load on the buses that you will find waiting outside. Don't worry about your baggage. Our people are getting it off now, and you will pick it up at the replacement center. Okay, that's it for now. Let's move off the aircraft!"

The men in the cabin rose as one to obey the sergeant's instruction. There was no talking now; each of them was wrapped entirely in his own thoughts. Andy Cullen's heart was in his throat as he was carried along by the rapidly moving line. He ducked his head and stumbled through the open door of the aircraft. The air that enveloped him was so warm and moist, he felt as if he had entered a steam bath. He breathed in a greenhouse smell, tinged with wood smoke and a hint of corruption, like rotting garbage. There was something else too, something unpleasant that he could not quite put his finger on.

20

Pausing at the top of the mobile ramp, he took in his first view of the country of Viet Nam.

A light rain was materializing from a low-hanging mist, coating the perforated steel panels of the runway with gleaming moisture. Visibility was poor, but he could make out a cluster of makeshift buildings and tents sitting on a patch of red earth, and beyond, a shadowy wall of green. Pressure from the men behind him forced him on down the ramp. At the bottom one of the Air Force crew was standing.

"Don't walk under the wing," he called. "Don't walk under the wing!"

The plane's engines were still running, ready for a quick getaway. Their hot breath bathed him in kerosene exhaust fumes. He saw the waiting buses, then noticed the men who had ridden out in them to meet the plane. They stood behind a rope off to one side, and it was necessary to walk past them to get to the buses.

One in particular caught his eye: a blond-haired boy who, at first glance, might have been one of his high school classmates. He wore the Combat Infantryman's Badge and, in addition to the standard Viet Nam service ribbons, the Bronze Star, Purple Heart and Air Medal. Deeply tanned, he was as lean as a long-distance runner. His hair stuck out like straw beneath his overseas cap. A few good-natured jibes were hurled from behind the rope at the newcomers, but this boy did not join in the banter. His sky-blue eyes were fixed on Andy, but rather than seeing him, seemed to be looking right through him to some place light years away. The guy gave him the creeps. It seemed as if he has been caught in the wrong movie, one about zombies instead of soldiers.

He climbed aboard an olive drab bus and took a seat next to Ty, who had boarded ahead of him. In no time, the bus was full. The sergeant who addressed them on the plane swung himself up next to the driver and shouted:

"Everybody here Cav replacements? If you're not a Cav replacement, raise your hand. Good. This bus will take you to the repo depot. I'm not sure-"

The sergeant was interrupted by a tremendous roar of voices raised in a cheer. All eyes on the bus turned to see the men who had been waiting at the edge of the runway surge up the ramp of the C-141. The sergeant laughed.

"Don't start thinking about that now. You all have a long way to go, three hundred sixty-five days. Anyway, as I was saying, I'm not sure when we'll be able to get you on a flight to An Khe. An Air Cav battalion is in contact to the west of here, and all available aircraft are being used to carry troops and supplies. All I can promise is I'll try to get you out sometime today. In the meantime, well, we have tents."

The sergeant waved and jumped out, running to pass his information on to the next bus. As they started to roll, there came a scream of jet engines, and the C-141 transport streaked by, its wheels off the ground. In an instant it had vanished in the mist.

*

The rain had stopped, and the tent in which the replacements were waiting had become a sauna. An hour remained before they were due to report for their flight to An Khe, where the First Air Cavalry Division maintained its base camp. Ty was dozing again, his head pillowed on his duffel bag. Andy nudged him, none too gently, on the shoulder.

"What are you trying to do," he said, "sleep away your whole tour?"

"Jus' baggin' a few z's," Ty replied. "You know," he added, "you just might have somethin' dere, Andy. If Ah could jus' sleep fo' a year Ah could wake up back in the good ol' USA."

"If anybody can do it, you can. Hey, you know, it's stopped raining. What do you say we go outside and take a look around?"

"You go ahead, buddy. Ah think Ah'll jus' stay heah an' take it easy."

"Are you crazy? It must be a hundred and fifty degrees in here!"

"It ain't so bad. Ah got a feelin' any kahnd a roof ovuh ouah heads 'll look pretty good befo' long."

Shaking his head over his friend's laziness, Andy slipped out of the tent. Outside, the sky had brightened considerably. The sun was visible through the haze, small as a dime and painless to the eye. Near the concertina wire at the edge of the compound a group of Vietnamese were digging a ditch. He strolled in their direction, curious to catch his first glimpse of the natives of the country. As he drew nearer, he was surprised to realize that all of the workers were women. One in particular caught his eye. Younger and prettier than the others, she reminded him of France Nuyen in *South Pacific*. As she bent to chop at the earth with a hoe-like implement, her baggy pants tightened to reveal a distinctly feminine shape.

22

The old crone who was supervising the work detail (a reasonable facsimile of Bloody Mary) noticed him watching and came over to speak to him.

"GI go boom-boom?" she cackled.

"Yes," he replied happily, pantomiming the firing of a pistol with his thumb cocked and forefinger extended. "Boom-boom!"

They repeated the phrase to one another several times, nodding and laughing their agreement. When it became clear that this had exhausted their conversational resources, he waved goodbye and returned to the tent.

"Guess what," he exclaimed, rousing Ty again, "I just talked with a real Vietnamese person."

When he described his meeting with the old woman, Ty was less than enthusiastic.

"Big fuckin' deal, man. Ah don' care nuffin' 'bout some ol' Viennamese lady."

Ty's lack of interest in their new surroundings had annoyed Andy. Now his friend's attitude made him genuinely angry.

"What's the matter with you?" he shouted. "How can you say you don't care about these people?"

"Don't have nuffin' to do wid me," Ty insisted sullenly.

"Nothing to do with you? We're here to defend their country, and it's got nothing-"

While he was speaking, the tent flap was pulled back, and the very person they had been discussing poked her head inside. Her eyes lit up when she saw Andy. She entered the tent, pulling the girl that he had been watching along by the hand.

"GI gimme fi' hundid pee," she said.

Andy looked in consternation from the old woman to the girl. Viewed frontally, her face was wider than he had thought, but was still pretty. With a sickening turn of his stomach, he realized that she was blind in one eye. He could not bear to look at the clouded iris.

"Boom-boom," the woman insisted. "Fi' hundid pee."

It occurred to him that she was asking for money, perhaps to pay for medical treatment for the unfortunate girl. But he had no Vietnamese currency, and their briefing at Travis had included a stern admonition against giving greenbacks to the natives. He smiled and shrugged helplessly. This produced an angry and unintelligible stream of words. He turned to Ty, who was smiling from ear to ear.

"What do I do now?" he asked. "She seems to be asking for mon-

23

ey, but I don't have any I can give her."

The other soldiers in the tent had been watching the little drama with interest. A buck sergeant whose ribbons indicated that this was his second tour in-country piped up:

"Hey, man, ain't you figured it out yet? All this 'boom-boom' talk ain't about shooting. Mama-san here thinks you made a deal for the young lady's services. Five hundred pee is only five bucks. Why don't you take her up on it?"

His words were greeted with general laughter. Andy felt the hot color flood his face.

"No, no," he protested, shaking his head vehemently. "Big mistake, no boom-boom."

The old woman looked at him with profound disgust.

"You cheap Charlie," she spat. "Numbah ten!"

Taking the girl's hand, she led her from the tent. Surrounded by gales of laughter, Andy sat down on his duffel bag and turned his face to the wall.

*

With his handlebar moustache, sunglasses and shoulder holster, the pilot of the CV-2 Caribou looked like he had just stepped off the set of a World War II movie. Strapped in the cargo seats amid cardboard boxes, lumber and pallets of artillery rounds, the Cav replacements hung nervously on his every word.

"It'll be a rough ride," he told them. "I keep her close to the deck to avoid ground fire. But it's a short hop to Camp Radcliff, only about fifteen minutes. We'll leave the loading ramp open part way, so it won't get too stuffy. If you think you're going to lose your lunch, use one of those paper bags that are on the seats. If you mess up the aircraft, you buy the ground crew a case of beer."

He waved and headed for the cockpit, and moments later the plane began to vibrate with the throb of its twin engines. Two young crew members took their seats, donning headsets, as the Caribou lumbered down the runway, its wheels bumping over the uneven surface. The plane turned around, and the engines roared as they began their takeoff roll. To Andy, who had grown accustomed to the power of the jet transport, it felt as if the straining propellers would not be able to lift them from the ground. He breathed a sigh of relief when, with a shuddering lurch, they became airborne.

As promised, it was a bumpy flight. The sensation of following the contours of the terrain at a low altitude was like riding in a small boat on a rough sea. Through the open tailgate, Andy caught fleeting glimpses of an exotic landscape: a village of thatch-roofed huts, rows of cultivated bushes, a farmer and a water buffalo craning their necks skyward in surprise. He realized that the pilot's method of avoiding ground fire was effective. They would be hit only if they were unlucky enough to pass directly over someone who was ready and waiting; and if that happened, they would be difficult to miss. Noticing that the flight crew were sitting on folded flak vests, he felt his scrotum tighten.

All signs of civilization were quickly left behind. They soared above a range of mountains blanketed with a dense forest canopy, and swooped down over a plateau where the vegetation was sparse and brown mingled with the various shades of green. Glancing at his watch, Andy realized that their trip was almost over. The speed with which they had traveled from Pleiku, near the Cambodian border, to a point midway to the coast brought home to him how small a country Viet Nam really was.

The plane climbed sharply and went into a steep, banking turn. Ty tapped him on the shoulder and jerked his thumb to the rear. A mountain had come into view behind them. Almost perfectly round, it perched on the flatter terrain that surrounded it like a blister. At its crest was a broad swatch of color. Andy recognized the yellow shield with the black diagonal stripe and horse head that was the emblem of the First Air Cavalry Division. Altering the very face of the landscape to announce the division's presence seemed an incredibly audacious thing to do. He felt a surge of pride to be joining a group of men who were capable of such bravado.

The pilot set the plane down as neatly as if it were the fighter for which he probably yearned. While the cargo was being unloaded, Andy stood off to one side with the other replacements, taking in his first view of Camp Radcliff. The edge of the runway was crowded with aircraft, primarily the helicopters for which the First Air Cav was famous. There were H-13's, the glass bubbles with erector set tails used for observation, giant Sikorsky flying cranes, CH-47 "Chinook" transports, and of course the UH-1D's, the "Hueys" which were the horses that the modern cavalry rode into battle. Mechanics swarmed over the machines like ants, their movements conveying a sense of urgency. Here and there, clouds of red dust swirled around helicopters

25

whose engines were being tested by their ground crews.

Departures and arrivals were occurring at a frequency that would have strained the capacity of a major American airport. Scanning the sky, Andy saw several Hueys flying together in formation. Farther off toward the horizon, a Chinook was making its way homeward with the broken carcass of a Huey slung below it, rotor bent and tail askew.

The airstrip was bordered by a wide grassy area, beyond which a dense concentration of tents and unpainted wooden buildings could be seen. Trucks and jeeps moved along busy thoroughfares, hurrying to the accomplishment of unknown purposes. Andy had no clear picture of what he had expected base camp to be like, entertaining vague notions of a remote jungle outpost. The thriving metropolis that he saw before him was far beyond anything that he had envisioned.

"It's a fuckin' city," Ty said, expressing his own thoughts exactly.

A two-and-a-half-ton truck came speeding toward them along the side of the runway, its wheels kicking up dust in spite of the rain that continued to fall. It stopped with a metallic squeal of worn brakes, and the young driver rolled down the window and stuck his head outside.

"What are you waiting for, cherries?" he yelled. "Get in!"

The replacements threw their duffel bags into the back of the truck and scrambled in after them. The deuce-and-a-half lurched into a U-turn and started back in the direction from which it had come. They were travelling along a well-graded dirt road that circled the inside of the camp's perimeter. Andy could see the tops of watchtowers manned by soldiers with machine guns. They passed motor pools, supply depots, a field hospital, a battery of 105-millimeter howitzers resting in sandbagged emplacements. Signs proclaimed the designations of various units: infantry, artillery, engineer, signal, transportation, military police. In front of an infantry battalion's headquarters, a scoreboard provided a running total of enemy killed in action and listed by name the recipients of various decorations.

The truck dropped the men off in an open area behind a long, one-storey wooden structure. They stood in a row with their duffel bags and AWOL bags in front of them, as the rain soaked through their khaki uniforms and puddled at their feet. It seemed an eternity, but was probably not more than five minutes, before a door opened and a rangy, jut-jawed drill sergeant type wearing crisp fatigues and spit-shined jungle boots stepped out to address them.

"Men," he said, "welcome to the First Team. My name is Sergeant Howell, and I am responsible for your in-processing. You men can be proud to be joining the most effective fighting force in the history of warfare, the First Cavalry Division (Airmobile). You are going to become Skytroopers. Your stay with me will be short, because our units are all undermanned, and need you ASAP. We will process your paperwork and give you a brief orientation on the First Cav and some 'dos' and 'don'ts' for your tour of duty in-country. Please pay careful attention to the briefings. I am not exaggerating when I say that what you are told here could save your life."

Sergeant Howell looked at his watch.

"It is now one-four hundred hours, local time. I want you all to go to the barracks building next door and find a bunk. Change into your fatigue uniform and report back here at fourteen-thirty with three copies of your orders. Any questions? Good. Dis-missed!"

IV. LAND OF THE TWO-WAY FIRING RANGE

Standing in one of the lines leading up to the tables where clerks were processing the papers of the replacements, Andy decided that this was just the same as being in the stateside Army: Go here, go there, hurry up and wait. The line moved slowly, which was fine with him, as they were no longer standing in the rain.

By eavesdropping on the conversations occurring ahead of him, he figured out that all of the replacements in this group were being assigned to companies of the First Battalion, Sixth Cavalry, and that the assignments were being made alphabetically based upon the first letter of the last name. In spite of the difference between their names, he came up with a scheme to get himself sent to the same company as his friend Ty.

The line had moved to the point at which only one man stood between him and the table. The hulking farm boy ahead of him told the clerk that his name was Danielson, and handed over his orders. The clerk stamped the orders, placed two copies into different files and handed the third copy back to Danielson.

"A-1-6," he said. "Present this copy of your orders when you report to company headquarters."

"'A-1-6,'" Danielson repeated. "Is that an aviation unit?"

"Hell, no," the clerk answered with a laugh, "that's an infantry company."

"But I'm a helicopter mechanic. You can't assign me to an infantry company."

"I don't assign nobody nowhere," said the clerk. "I just do what

29

I'm told, and what I'm told is, everybody here goes to the First of the Sixth."

"But that's a mistake," Danielson protested, shaking visibly as he began to realize what was happening to him. "I was promised-"

"Look," the clerk said in a tone that indicated that his patience was being sorely tried, "there ain't nothing I can do about it. You have been assigned to Alpha Company, First of the Sixth. You got a problem, take it up with your company commander. Next!"

The clerk glared at Andy as he stepped up next to poor Danielson, who was still standing there staring dumbly at the orders in his hand. The timing was bad, but he decided to give it his best shot anyway.

"PFC Andrew T. Cullen," he announced, handing the clerk his orders. "That's 'T. Cullen,' he added, with a 'T.'"

The clerk looked down at the orders, then up at Andy.

"Don't you mean 'Cullen,' with a 'C,' 'Andrew T.?'"

"You got me," Andy laughed, raising his hands in surrender. "Look," he said in a confidential tone, "all I'm trying to do is get assigned to the same company as my buddy, Clarence Tyree. We went through basic and AIT together, and it would be great if we can stay together now. You can just switch me with one of the other guys. What do you say?"

"Jesus Christ," the clerk snarled, "I never heard so much Mickey Mouse bullshit. All of you guys want special treatment. What do you think this is, Sunday school?"

He stamped the orders with vehement finality.

"A-1-6. Next!"

*

The rain was coming down now in earnest, drumming on the canvas tarp that covered the back of the deuce-and-a-half and running down the sides in torrents. The truck's engine whined in low gear, as its wheels churned through the quagmire of the perimeter road. Huddled on the wooden benches in the back, the replacements wore hooded ponchos over their fatigue uniforms. Cold and hungry and sleep-deprived, they had spent the past three days learning about the myriad ways in which death could be found here in "the Land of the Two-Way Firing Range." With visions of malaria, cholera and plague, punji sticks, RPG's and satchel charges dancing through their heads, they were now on the last leg of their journey, the one that would deliver them to their assigned units.

After turning onto a side road and proceeding a short distance, the truck ground to a halt. The driver rolled down his window, stuck his head out and shouted:

"A-1-6! All of you cherries assigned to Alpha Company, this is your stop!"

Andy and the other five Alpha Company replacements lurched to their feet. Danielson was the first over the tailgate, and he reached up to take the others' luggage. As the men piled out, Ty gave Andy's arm a squeeze. The last thing he saw as the truck pulled away was his friend smiling and waving at him.

They were standing at the beginning of a gravel walk bordered by white-painted stones, leading up to the entrance to a GP medium tent. Next to the entrance was a sign proclaiming this to be Alpha Company's headquarters. The rain was coming down hard, and they wasted no time in scurrying up the pathway and through the entrance.

Inside two clerks, one black and the other white, were banging away at typewriters. They were young and frail-looking, and except for their color, were as alike as a pair of bookends. Seated at a rickety table, a game of solitaire laid out before him, was a tiny gargoyle of a man with silver hair and skin the color of mahogany. At the sight of the new arrivals, his ugly features split into a grin.

"Christmas!" he exclaimed. "It must be Christmas! Look what Santa Claus has brought us. Six, count 'em, six, new men. Welcome to Alpha Company, men. I am First Sergeant Emilio Sanchez, and your ass now belongs to me."

The first sergeant spread his arms wide in a gesture of welcome.

"Don't be shy, men. You have a copy of your orders with you, yes? Step right up here, and let's have a look at them."

The young men obediently formed a line in front of the first sergeant's desk. Danielson was the first to hand over his orders.

"Where are you from, young man?"

"Iowa, first sergeant."

"Bet you've stacked some hay in your time, yes?"

"Only about a zillion bales, first sergeant."

"Danielson, you were made to carry a mortar tube. I'm assigning you to the Weapons Platoon."

"Permission to speak, first sergeant."

"What is it, Danielson?"

"If you check my 201 File, you'll see my MOS is Sixty-Seven November, helicopter repairman. The First Cav needs helicopter repairmen, first sergeant. With respect, first sergeant, I shouldn't be carrying a mortar tube."

"You got a point there, Danielson." First Sergeant Sanchez pulled on his chin, pursed his lips, drummed his fingers on the table. "Tell you what I'll do: I'll send a note up to Battalion HQ and make them aware of your situation. For now, though, you go where I tell you. *Comprende?*"

"Yes, first sergeant. Thank you."

Danielson moved off to one side, and another man stepped up to the table. The first sergeant assigned him to the First Platoon, the next man to the Second, and the man after him to the Third. The man ahead of Andy, a New York City black by the name of Briscoe, was told to report to First Platoon. Bringing up the rear, Andy was about to hand over his orders when the growl of a jeep engine sounded outside, and the crunch of footsteps could be heard on the gravel path. A white-helmeted MP poked his dripping head and shoulders inside the tent.

First Sergeant Sanchez? We've got a prisoner to deliver."

All of the lines and creases in the first sergeant's face crinkled in an expression of pure, malevolent delight. He jumped up from his chair scattering cards and documents off the table.

"It's about time! We were expecting him two days ago."

"Yeah, this weather has slowed everything down. Wait a minute, we'll bring him in."

The white helmet withdrew, and moments later, a manacled prisoner came into the tent flanked by burly MP's. Built like an NFL linebacker, he was dressed like a Vietnamese peasant, in black pajamas and crude rubber sandals. His dark hair had grown into a tangle of unruly curls. His face was a mess: nose and upper lip split and caked with dried blood, one eye purple and swollen shut, a golf ball-sized lump on his forehead. He held his damaged head high as he gazed coolly at the first sergeant with his one good eye.

"Horvath," said the first sergeant, "it's good to see you, my friend. Did you enjoy your little vacation?"

"If you'll just sign for the prisoner," one of the MP's put in, "we'll be on our way."

"Certainly I'll sign for him," said the first sergeant, taking the proffered clipboard. "Arthur!" he snapped, causing one of the clerks to jump to attention. "Take these new men to their billets."

The clerk took a raincoat and cap from a coat rack and motioned to the replacements to follow him. As the only one who had not yet received his assignment, Andy was unsure whether or not to go with the group. He decided to stay behind.

"We'll take the cuffs off him now, okay?"

The first sergeant gestured his assent, and the MP produced a key and removed the manacles from the prisoner's wrists and ankles. Andy edged instinctively away. He had no idea what this character had done, and did not want to be near if violence should erupt. Happily, his concern proved to be unfounded. The man that the first sergeant called "Horvath" stood quietly, rubbing his wrists, as the two MP's departed.

"Horvath," said the first sergeant, "The CO will decide whether to give you an Article 15 hearing or a summary court martial. Until then you are restricted to quarters at all times unless you are at chow or on work detail. Now you ain't going to get squirrelly on me, are you?"

"No, Top. I'll behave myself."

"Good. Get yourself cleaned up and get a haircut and report back here in proper uniform at 1100 hours. Now, who the hell are you?"

Andy was startled to realize that the first sergeant's glare was focused upon him. He approached the table, holding out his orders.

"First sergeant, PFC Cullen reports."

The first sergeant snatched the paper from him and scanned it.

"You're one of the replacements. Why weren't you with the others?"

Andy did not know what to say to that. To his relief, the clerk who had remained in the tent piped up:

"He was here with the others, Top. You just didn't get to him before Horvath showed up."

Andy made a mental note to buy this guy a beer.

"All right," the first sergeant growled. "Cullen, you're assigned to Third Platoon. Go with Horvath here, and he'll show you where to bunk. Then report back here with him at 1100 hours. Dismissed!"

*

The barracks was a long building of fresh lumber with a cement floor and a corrugated metal roof. Screening had been installed below the eaves to provide ventilation. The open floor plan was divided into identical living spaces, each consisting of a cot with mosquito netting rigged over it and standard Army wall and foot lockers. Bare electric light bulbs dangled at intervals on cords from the ceiling. A couple of these were burning, courtesy of a gasoline-powered generator that could be heard chugging away outside.

"All the comforts of home," Andy said admiringly.

"This is Third Platoon's hooch," Horvath told him. "Those bunks over there are empty. You want to take one on the west side, because the rain can blow in through the screen when it gets windy."

Following Horvath's advice, Andy dropped his duffel bag onto a cot on the side that he had indicated. He took out his damp khakis and hung them in the wall locker, stowed his low quarter shoes which were already growing a coat of green mold. On the inside of the door of the locker hung a crude hand-written calendar. All but the last few days had been crossed out. At the bottom, the acronym, "DEROS," was scrawled in large capital letters.

"What's this mean?" he asked.

"That's what we call a 'short-timer's calendar,'" Horvath replied. "It shows the number of days a guy has got left in his tour. 'DEROS' stands for, 'date of estimated return from overseas.'"

"So the guy went home?"

"Well, you might say that. Roy went back to the World in a box."

Andy was startled by the voice coming from beneath the mosquito netting on a neighboring bunk. The netting was raised, and a pair of skinny legs swung out, followed by an unshaven, chinless face that blinked at the new arrivals.

"Horvath," the man said, "what the fuck are you doing here? You're supposed to be on in-country R and R. What happened to you, man? You look like hell."

"Hi Snake," Horvath answered with a laugh. "It's good to see you too. My R and R got cut short. I tangled with some Vietnamese rangers in Nha Trang in a fight over a bar girl. Fucked a couple of 'em up pretty good. The MP's brought me back in manacles."

"That's tough, man. They gonna throw the book at you?"

"Aw, they'll probably just bust me back to private again. They need bodies too bad to send me to the Big Max. Hope I can get out to the boonies soon, though. Top will make it pretty rough for me here in base camp. How come you're here, Snake?"

34

"The whole company is back in base camp. We got rotated in from the field to pull perimeter guard duty. I got a pass to go into Alpha Kilo this afternoon."

"Looks like you got started on your fun a little early."

"Damn straight!" Snake exclaimed.

Lurching to his feet, he staggered to his wall locker and took a can of Pabst Blue Ribbon off the top. He zipped off the tab and dropped it into the open can. He tilted his head back, and his Adam's apple bobbed up and down as he guzzled the beer.

"Ulp-aaaaah!"

Snake hurled the empty can away. As it rattled on the floor, he reached for another. Thin to the point of emaciation, his thinness emphasized the plumpness of the genitals dangling like ripe fruit between his scrawny thighs.

"Snake," said Horvath, "say hello to Andy Cullen, the newest member of Third Platoon. Andy, this is Snake Holloway, my good buddy from the Third Squad."

The thin man turned and fixed upon Andy his bleary scrutiny. At ten o'clock in the morning, he was obviously drunk.

"Welcome to hell, cherry," he said.

"Hell has its privileges," Horvath said cheerfully. "Hey, Snake, why don't you take Andy along with you this afternoon?"

"Yeah, sure. Just what I need, a fuckin' new guy to cramp my style."

"Cramp your style, Snake, a cocksman like you? Come on! You're the best one to show a new guy the ropes. All the gals down in Sin City love you."

"You got that right," said Snake, preening under Horvath's flattery. "After they get over the size of my root, anyway. Scares 'em at first."

"Look, Snake, I'd take him downtown myself, but I'm restricted to base until they decide what they're going to do with me. Do this for me, okay? I'll owe you."

"You got that right," Snake said again, apparently liking the ring of that phrase. "You and him both. All right, cherry, meet me at the motor pool at fifteen hundred hours. If you're one minute late, I'm going without you."

"He'll be there," said Horvath. "Thanks, buddy."

*

"What does he mean, 'cherry?'" Andy asked Horvath. "Why is everybody calling me that?"

They were traveling in a three-quarter-ton truck loaded with cut-off 55-gallon drums, each of which contained several inches of kerosene that they had picked up at the motor pool.

"Man," Horvath replied, "you really are a cherry, ain't you? 'Cherry' means, 'virgin,' like you say, 'I busted her cherry,' okay?"

Andy felt his ears turning cherry red. He was in fact a virgin, but it seemed impossible that these guys could know it just by looking at him.

"But here," Horvath continued, "we use it to refer to a guy who ain't been in combat yet. You ain't really been fucked, man, until you been in combat."

"Oh," said Andy, greatly relieved, "I get it."

"Let me tell you something though," said Horvath. "By the time the first sergeant gets through with us, we're gonna wish we was in the boonies. Shit-burning detail is the worst, man."

"What does it mean, 'shit-burning detail?'"

"What you think it means? It means we burn the shit, that's what. Look, I don't know how many men we got here at Camp Radcliff, but it's gotta be at least fifteen thousand, right? If each guy dumps a load of, say, one pound each day, that means like seven-and-a-half tons of shit every day. Man, that's one hell of a lotta shit. Think about it: What are you going to do with all that shit? Bury it? Cart it off somewhere? Some genius had the bright idea of burning it. It goes up in smoke. Presto, no more shit!"

"Omigod. You've got to be shitting me."

"Hah! I shit you not. Of course the smoke from all this burning smells like, well, shit. Haven't you noticed that the air smells kinda funny around here?"

Andy recalled the odor that he was unable to identify when he first stepped off the plane. He realized that it had continually been present, but that he had grown used to it and no longer noticed it. Learning what he had been breathing in on a constant basis made him feel slightly nauseated.

After passing First Battalion headquarters, Horvath pulled the truck over next to a shower building that had a tank with an immersion heater on the roof. Adjoining the building was a smaller screened-in shed.

"This is our first stop," Horvath said, "the officers' latrine. It's a six-holer. Lucky for us officers' shit don't stink."

Hinged panels at the bottom of the latrine provided access to the drums that rested beneath the holes inside. Andy helped Horvath pull them out and replace them with fresh drums from the truck. They loaded the full drums in the back of the truck, and Horvath drove them to an open area at the western edge of their brigade's sector.

"We use this place," Horvath explained, "because the wind is mainly from the southeast at this time of year and it blows the smoke over to the First of the Seventh. It don't matter much, though, because other units are doing the same-same thing to us."

They donned heavy gloves and dragged the drums full of officers' shit out into the middle of a patch of bare dirt. Horvath produced a book of matches and dropped a lighted match into each of the drums. The kerosene immediately caught fire, sending up orange flames and boiling clouds of thick black smoke. When the flames died down after a minute or two, they stirred the bubbling, noxious mixture with steel rods to ensure thorough burning. Proximity to the fire quickly caused their clothes to become saturated with the awful stench.

"Bet you never thought you'd be doing this when you came to the Nam," Horvath said with a laugh.

"You aren't kidding!" Andy replied. "This makes me wish I'd taken my CO's advice after basic training and applied to Officer Candidate School."

"You could have gone to OCS?"

"Well, yeah. I was in my second year of college when I dropped out and enlisted."

"You had a college deferment, and you dropped out? You gotta be kidding."

"It seemed like being there didn't make any sense. Not when the biggest thing that might ever happen in my lifetime was going on, and I wasn't a part of it."

"That 'big thing,' of course, being Viet Nam."

"Yeah, right."

"And you enlisted."

"Actually, I volunteered for the draft, a two-year commitment. That's the main reason I decided not to do OCS; it would have meant another year."

"And you chose to be an Eleven Bravo."

"Yep."

"And you volunteered for the Nam."

Andy shrugged his shoulders and held his palms up in a gesture of surrender.

"Guilty."

Listen, Andy, I'm gonna to give you a piece of advice, and you damn well better follow it. Don't tell nobody else what you just told me. Do you hear me, nobody. Not the part about college, not the part about OCS, not the part about volunteering. Do you hear me, cherry?"

"Yeah, I hear you, but-"

"No buts! Just do like I say. Guys here, they ain't gonna understand why anybody would do what you done. And they ain't gonna like it. You hear me?"

"Yeah, okay."

"Now I'm gonna tell you something: I volunteered for this shithole too. I was born in Hungary. I was nine years old when my family escaped and came to America. How old are you, Andy?"

"Twenty."

"That makes us the same age then. What do you know about the Hungarian revolution?"

"Not very much, I'm afraid."

"That makes two of us. I was very young. What I remember is standing in front of a barn with my family and Russian soldiers pointing their rifles at us. The look on my father's face was something I won't ever forget. It was like he was de-balled, you know?"

"Yeah, I guess so."

"I grew up hating communists, and when Viet Nam came along, there was Anton Horvath trotting down to the recruitment center to enlist. I was in the Eleventh Air Assault Test Division at Fort Benning, which became the First Air Cav. I came over on the Buckler, the first troop ship that left the States in August of Sixty-Five. I was at Happy Valley, LZ X-Ray, Bong Son, Operation Masher and White Wing. I got my chance to kill boo-coo communists. And Charlie got plenty of chances to kill me."

"But you're still here."

"Am I? Sometimes I wonder about that, I really do. Let me tell you something, Andy: The Nam changes you. In another month, you ain't hardly gonna remember the guy you are today. I guaran-fucking-tee it. You are gonna meet somebody that's been living inside a you

38

and you don't even know it."

What kind of talk was this? It seemed to Andy that Horvath was being overly dramatic. To be sure, he was tough, hardened by his experience; but he seemed fundamentally normal. Andy believed that he knew himself, and doubted that any huge surprises were in store. He just hoped that the person living inside him did not turn out to be a coward.

*

"Sin City, here we come!"

Showered, shaved and dressed in clean and pressed fatigues, Snake Holloway looked almost presentable. He steered the jeep that they had picked up at the motor pool one-handed, a Camel dangling from his lip, as he regaled his nervous passenger with tales of the "good old days."

"You ain't gonna believe this place, cherry. A whole town of nothing but bars and whorehouses, full of sweet, tight young pussy at just five bucks a pop. It used to be that when we went to the ville, we had to wear a steel pot and carry a weapon with ammo, 'cause you never knew when Charlie was gonna crash the party. It was called 'Dodge City' back then. Shootouts were always happening with the ARVN and between guys from different units. Finally the brass figured out that we were more of a danger to each other than Charlie was. Now only MP's carry weapons in Sin City."

They joined a procession of vehicles stopping at the main gate of Camp Radcliff, where an MP checked their passes and waved them through. After passing through the perimeter defenses, they came to a shanty town where crude dwellings had been constructed with cardboard, scrap lumber and whatever other materials were available. Even beer and soft drink cans had been flattened and used as shingles for roofing and siding, an ingenious as well as colorful expedient.

"Those are refugee hooches," Snake explained. "Vietnamese who've been relocated from the free-fire zones living next to our base camp for handouts, and protection too, I guess."

A few people could be seen moving about in the refugee camp. As the jeep passed by, Andy caught a glimpse of a naked, potbellied toddler; an old woman with betel nut-stained teeth; two girls sitting front-to-back, as one parsed the other's hair with her fingers.

"Head lice," said Snake, seeing the direction in which he was looking. "Ever hear the expression, 'nit-picking?' Well, there you have it."

An old man wearing a conical hat was walking along the road in the direction in which they were traveling. As they drew even with him, he dropped the trousers of his black pajamas and squatted by the roadside.

"Is he doing what I think he is?" Andy asked.

"Damn straight," Snake replied. "Them zipperheads shit any-place they feel like, like fuckin' dogs."

They turned onto a paved road that Snake told him was a section of Highway 19, which ran all the way from Pleiku near the Cambodian border to the seaport of Qui Nhon. They entered an area that Snake referred to as "new An Khe," where crude stalls had been constructed along the highway, almost like a shopping mall.

"Anything you want is for sale here," Snake announced proudly. "Ain't nothing you can't buy. Except maybe a round-eyed gal."

They passed barbershops, laundries, souvenir and sundry stores. Andy could not help but notice that many of the goods on display were government-issue military equipment. He decided not to comment on this, or ask how such items had come to be offered for sale. They came to some shacks with signs advertising the availability of steam baths and massage.

"This," Snake said, "is where you go if you want a steam job and blow bath. We ain't stopping here today. I wanna get laid one last time before I'm PCOD. We're going to Sin City."

"'P C...?"

"Pussy cut-off date, man. Got a ticket on the Freedom Bird! Can't be going back to the Land of the Big PX with a dose of the clap, and I only got eighteen days and a wake-up."

Sin City turned out to be a compound of recently constructed buildings surrounded by a high barbed wire fence. Snake asked the MP in reflecting sunglasses who checked their i.d.'s if he would mind watching their jeep for an hour or so.

"Sure," the MP replied. "You guys go ahead."

A steady stream of foot traffic was passing through the gate. Many of the soldiers coming in the opposite direction were obviously drunk, stumbling along with their arms around their buddies' shoulders. "Dodge City" was a good name for this place. The muddy street lined with wooden sidewalks and crude saloons could have served as the set for an Old West movie. Brushing off a small boy peddling condoms,

Snake led Andy through the entrance of an establishment whose exterior was painted robin's-egg blue, and whose sign proclaimed it to be the "Houston Bar." The barroom was not crowded. As his eyes grew accustomed to the dim lighting, Andy saw only three or four groups of soldiers sitting with women at tables, laughing and talking in subdued tones. There was a pungent odor in the air, and even though he had never smelled it before, he was certain that it was marijuana. As he watched, a couple detached itself from one of the groups and disappeared through a bamboo-curtained doorway.

Snake led the way to a vacant table and called loudly for beer. Almost immediately a girl appeared, carrying bottles of beer and glasses on a tray. Tall for a Vietnamese, she was dressed in tight blue capri pants and a yellow halter top that showed off a truly stupendous body. As she approached their table, Andy saw that her face was pleasant, but somewhat horsey, and that her hair was reddish and frizzy. He realized that she was probably of mixed race.

"Frenchie!" Snake greeted her. "How ya doing, honey? Long time no see."

"Hi, GI," the girl replied, baring long, yellowish teeth. "You buy me tea?"

"What's this 'GI' stuff, Frenchie? Don't you remember your old pal, Snake?"

"Oh sure I memba. How it hanging, big boy?"

"Hanging just fine, honey."

Catching the girl around the waist, Snake pulled her onto his lap. She did not resist, but laughed and draped an arm about his neck.

"You buy me tea?" she repeated.

Ignoring the question, Snake slipped a hand between Frenchie's thighs and began to massage her crotch. With the other hand he raised his bottle in salute.

"How about this, eh, cherry? Is this the life or what?"

Andy had never before been in the presence of such openly lewd behavior, and he found it acutely embarrassing. Averting his eyes from the fingers that were now probing the cleft that was plainly visible in the tight capri pants, he smiled weakly and took a drink. The beer was icy cold and delicious, and it went instantly to his head. He felt suddenly carefree and irresponsible.

"You no buy me tea," Frenchie pouted. "You cheap Charlie!"

"Aw, don't get your panties in a wad, honey," Snake told her. "You got a couple boom-boom customers here. But first get us another beer like a good girl. And bring back some company for my friend here. He's a big hero. Kill boo-coo VC."

"Hero cute boy," Frenchie simpered. "Come back soon with pretty girl for Hero."

She jumped up from Snake's lap and sashayed off, ostentatiously shifting her plump bottom.

"Oh man," Snake crowed, following her with his eyes, "ain't that sweet? I'll tell you, man, that's one thing I'm gonna miss. Gals back in the World think they're such hot shit, ain't none of them can hold a candle to these gals here. These gals really know how to treat a man. Uh-oh, cherry, look what's coming."

Frenchie was returning, bringing fresh bottles of beer and followed by a slim figure in white cotton pajamas which were not tight, but were more form-fitting than the standard peasant variety. Andy's breath caught in his throat. The girl was pretty, no, more than pretty, lovely. Her skin was the color of honey, the hair hanging to her waist a glossy crow-black. Her face was heart-shaped, with prominent cheekbones and a small rosebud mouth. As she raised her almond eyes demurely to look at him, he rose involuntarily to his feet.

"Allo, GI," she said, in a small voice, "my name Lee. What yours?"

"Andy," he managed, through a throat constricted by shyness.

"Ahn-dee," she repeated. "That nice name."

He pulled out a chair for her, and she sat down beside him.

"You buy me tea?" she asked.

"Sure," he answered her, "anything you want."

He spoke the literal truth. In that moment, were it in his power, he would have bought her anything in the world that she might desire. At a neighboring table, a cheer erupted, as a young soldier emerged from the back rooms with one arm around a girl in a UCLA tee shirt and the other raised in a clenched fist salute.

Tilting the bottle high, Snake drained the last of his second beer. With a loud belch he slammed the empty bottle on the table and wiped the foam from his lips with the back of his hand.

"If you'll excuse us, Frenchie and I have a little bidness to attend to."

Snake grabbed Frenchie by the wrist and dragged her none too gently toward the curtained doorway. Although Andy had not seen Lee give any signal, a wizened little man wearing a white apron materialized and placed a small glass in front of her. She raised the glass and took a delicate sip.

Andy took a long pull on his second beer. Could this really be happening? He was Lieutenant Cable in *South Pacific,* and she was as beautiful as France Nuyen, no, even more beautiful. Girls had never found Andy unattractive. The reason that he still carried the shameful burden of virginity was that he was an incurable romantic, and had always set his sights too high. He had a strong suspicion that his luck was about to change.

"So," he said, groping for a conversational topic, "how long have you been working here?"

"Me new girl," Lee replied. "FNG," she added with a giggle.

He was unfamiliar with the acronym, but was unwilling to admit his ignorance.

"You're very pretty." *Gosh, Andy, what a smooth talker you are!*

"You not so bad yourself, GI. You have sweetheart back in Worl'?"

A good question. He wondered if Joan Munson qualified.

"Sure," he said.

"Lee make you not so lonesome, yes?"

She leaned closer to him, and the sweet, musky smell of her made him feel lightheaded. As her fingers gently brushed his cheek and slid around to the nape of his neck, her touch brought a sensation like a faint electric current. He was grateful for the semi-darkness, in which he hoped she would not notice the way the current was lighting up his ears. He was experiencing another reaction too, one that was even more embarrassing.

"Ahn-dee go boom-boom now?"

He jumped, as her fingertips brushed the swelling in his trousers. It was now or never. He was sure that every eye in the room was on him as he rose to follow her. They passed through the bamboo curtain and along a dark corridor with doors on either side. Lee opened a door, and they entered a small cubicle whose only furnishings were a bunk bed and a washstand with a basin of water and a folded towel resting on its top. High on the wall, a crude carving of the crucified Jesus gazed down upon the proceedings with love and compassion.

Lee helped him with the buttons on his fatigues, which his own fingers had become too clumsy to deal with. As she removed his shirt, she touched the puckered scar on his shoulder.

"VC?" she inquired.

The injury had occurred when he was riding his bicycle at age twelve and hit a patch of sand. As he rolled on the pavement, the bicycle's fender had dug a chunk of flesh out of his shoulder. Remembering the pain, he now shrugged and offered what he hoped was a manly smile.

"You my brave GI."

Lee led Andy to the bed, and when he sat, unlaced his boots and pulled them off along with his trousers, leaving him in only his green underwear and socks. Next she took off the white pajamas, stepping daintily out of the bottoms and draping them on the washstand. Unclothed, her body was revealed to be perfection in miniature, with surprisingly full breasts and a tiny waist swelling to rounded hips and thighs. Pushing him back onto the bare mattress, she lay down beside him. As he started to roll on top of her, she stopped him with a hand on his chest.

"Wait, Ahn-dee."

Opening a drawer in the washstand, she took out a foil-wrapped condom. How stupid of him, not to think of that himself. As she unrolled it on him, the touch of her fingers was almost more than he could bear. She turned onto her back and opened herself to him.

"Okay now, GI."

Trembling with nervousness and lust, he placed himself between her upraised knees and thrust into her. At the instant of contact, a dart struck through his lower abdomen. For a long moment he was held, transfixed, at the peak of sweet agony, before emptying himself in a series of helpless spasms.

*

"So, how was she?" Snake asked, as they rode together in the jeep back through the ville. "Number one boom-boom?"

Although proud of himself, Andy was plagued by a niggling doubt. It had all happened so fast, he was not absolutely certain that he had achieved penetration. Was he still a virgin, or was he not? He decided to give himself the benefit of the doubt.

"Snake," he said truthfully, "that was absolutely the finest piece of ass I ever had."

*

At the end of the day, Andy and Snake hitched a ride on the

chow truck out to the "Green Line," as the camp's perimeter was called, to relieve the other members of their squad on guard duty. They found them taking shelter from the rain in a heavily sandbagged bunker, three young-old men wearing filthy, rotting fatigues and cracked jungle boots. Andy noticed that, in spite of their ragged appearance, their rifles were spotless and gleamed with a light coat of oil. Their eyes glared at him from beneath the rims of their camouflaged steel pots with chilling intensity. He felt as if he had stumbled upon a den of wolves that had taken human form.

Snake introduced them: buck sergeant Bird Lawler, a rawboned Kentuckian who was the squad leader; Pete Rodriguez, slight of build and ferret-faced; and Jason Ash, startlingly white-complected, with pale blue eyes as lacking in affect as a doll's. As befitted his position, Sergeant Lawler was the first to speak.

"What the hell is he doing here?"

"Same as me," Snake replied. "Relieving you guys' sorry asses so you can go and take a shower and get drunk at the EM Club."

"But he ain't a member of Third Squad."

"He is now. Horvath requisitioned him."

"We don't need no fucking new guy."

"Come on, Bird, with Roy zapped, we're at only fifty percent strength. All of us are getting short, and I'm so short you can't hardly see me. Are we gonna wait until there ain't none of us left before we start bringing in new guys? Andy is okay, for a cherry. All you have to do is talk to Lt. Danforth to fix it up."

"Didn't you hear?" Bird said. "The LT ain't with us no more. Had an accident with a hand grenade."

Pete Rodriguez snickered. Jason Ash raised his eyes piously to the roof of the bunker.

"May he rest in peace."

"That ain't right," Snake exclaimed, visibly shocked. "That just ain't right! Lieutenant Danforth was a good leader."

"Some of the guys think he was too aggressive," said Bird. "Some of the guys…" and here he glanced quickly at Andy "…are glad he's gone."

"Aww, shit," said Snake. "I guess I'll take it up with the sarge, then. He'll probably be around sometime tonight."

"Maybe, if he can get his nose out of the whiskey bottle. Which reminds me," said Bird, "I've got some serious drinking to take care of myself. Come on, men, let's get out of here."

45

Sergeant Bird Lawler ducked through the door of the bunker, with Spec. 4's Rodriguez and Ash trailing behind him. As Ash passed by, he caught Andy's sleeve and pushed his face so close that Andy could feel the hot breath whispering in his ear.

"He sent you," Ash hissed, "didn't He?"

"What are you talking about," Andy replied. "Who sent me?"

But Ash had already disappeared.

*

The luminous dial of the Seiko watch that his father had given him as a high school graduation present told him that it was a quarter after midnight. Rain dripping from the sandbagged roof of the bunker provided a rhythmic accompaniment to the snuffling honks of Snake's snoring. From somewhere within the walls of the structure came the sounds of rats scurrying. Overhead the drone of a spotter plane could be heard, as it endlessly circled the base camp. Before lying down on a makeshift bed of ammo boxes and wrapping himself in his poncho liner, Snake had told him that there was no worse sin than falling asleep on sentry duty. Tired as he was, there was very little danger of that happening.

The war was providing sights and sounds that were more than adequate to keep him awake. Half a kilometer away, near the base of Hon Cong Mountain, a parachute flare drifted down, and beneath it a fountain of red tracers arced gracefully into the sky. Closer to his position, there came the flash-CRUMP! of a high-explosive artillery round impacting outside the wire. It was followed by a phosphorus round that burst open like a brilliant white flower. He was reminded of nights spent with friends on a hillside near his home, watching Fourth of July fireworks in the valley below. Oh, wow, look at that one! The difference, of course, was that these pyrotechnics had a deadly purpose.

After hours of staring into the blackness, his eyes were playing tricks on him. It did not matter that he was in a base so secure it could not be taken by a massed division. One of the things he had been taught during his orientation was that the Viet Cong sappers were capable of penetrating any position. While his brain told him that he must be mistaken, his eyes kept seeing shadows as enemy soldiers carrying satchel charges towards him through the wire.

As a boy he had been (like most kids, he supposed) afraid of the dark. His family's house had a long driveway, bordered by tall pines. When he had gone out at night to visit friends in his neighborhood, he had hated to go down that driveway, imagining that bogeymen lurked behind every tree. Leaving the circle of light that surrounded the porch, he would run like the wind, looking neither left nor right, until he reached the streetlight at the end of the driveway.

He remembered plainly the night on which he had conquered his fear. He had been on his way to see his best friend, Jimmy Briggs, and as usual had leapt from the porch and started out at top speed, running like a bat out of hell. Halfway down the driveway, something had caused him to stop. The hair on his neck had risen, as he had looked around at the dark shapes of the trees. A growl had started deep in his throat. Ducking behind the nearest tree, he had continued on, darting from tree to tree, until he had reached the end of the driveway. He no longer had to fear the bogeyman, for he had become the bogeyman.

Now the bogeymen in the darkness were real. They were out there somewhere, and they were bent on killing him. Struggling to get a grip on himself, he resorted to the same trick that had served him as a child. A growl rumbled low in his throat, and emerged as the fearsome cry that he had learned in basic training while thrusting a bayonet at dummies.

"Aaaargh!"

Awakened by his shout, Snake Holloway sat bolt upright, fumbling for his rifle.

"What the f-"

"Sorry," Andy said sheepishly, " Everything is okay. Go back to sleep."

Grumbling something about "goddamn cherries," Snake fell back and threw an arm over his eyes, and was instantly snoring again.

Andy had to laugh at himself; but, hey, if it worked, who was he to scoff? No longer a frightened child, the person peering out through the slit between the sandbags had become a fearsome killing machine. And what this killer heard with his highly sensitized ears was the sound of footsteps approaching the bunker. It was, of course, likely that this was some American walking along the perimeter; but he had been trained for this moment, and he knew exactly what to do. He snapped the loading handle of his brand new M-16, chambering a round.

"Halt!" he called. "Who is there?"

"Who the fuck is that?" a booming bass voice answered back.

It sounded like an American, but, as everyone knew, Charlie

47

could be very tricky. Andy did not want to shoot, but this was a war zone, and he was on sentry duty. He thought about waking up Snake, but there was no time. He decided to try something that he remembered from an old war movie.

"Who," he asked, "was the first Negro ballplayer in the big leagues?"

Before you could say "Jack Robinson," a bulky individual came into the bunker, bringing with him a potent reek of whiskey. He shook his poncho, spraying drops of moisture off him like a dog.

"Young man," he said in his deep voice, "stop pointing that weapon at me. Good. Now, move your selector switch to the 'safe' position. Good. Now, I'm asking you again, who the fuck are you and what are you doing in my bunker?"

It was too dark to see the man's rank, but from the sound of his voice, it was obvious that he was someone who considered himself to be important.

"I'm PFC Cullen, sir. I'm manning this bunker as a member of Third Squad, Third Platoon of Alpha Company, First of the Sixth."

"You don't 'sir' me, private. Last time I checked, I ain't been knighted by the queen. I am Sergeant First Class Roundtree, and I am the platoon sergeant and acting platoon leader of the Third Platoon. If you were a member of my platoon, I would know you, wouldn't I?"

"He's a new guy, sarge." This from Snake Holloway, who, thankfully, had awakened to join the discussion. "He just got here from Fort Benning a couple days ago. Top had him working details with Horvath- Horvath's back, did you know that- and we thought we could use him in Third Squad."

"Just what I fucking need after eleven months in-country, almost get blown away in base camp by a kid who's still pissing Fort Benning water. All of you guys in Third Squad are a bunch a fuck-ups, so this new guy should fit right in. But do me a favor, okay? Take the magazine out of his weapon and clear it, and make sure he don't shoot nobody tonight. Will you do that for me?"

"Sure, sarge, no problem."

Sergeant Roundtree went back out into the night. They heard him cursing when he stumbled over something as he continued down the line to check out the next position.

"Nice guy," Andy commented, when he was sure the sergeant was out of earshot.

"Yeah," Snake laughed, "you'd a made yourself the most popular guy in the platoon if you'd a zapped him. But then you wouldn't be with us long. They'd send you right down to LBJ."

"'LBJ'- what's that?"

"Long Binh Jail. The 'Big Max.' It's where they keep the real bad-asses. Put 'em in CONEX containers and only let 'em out an hour a day for exercise. Hey, what are you doing that for?"

Andy had removed the magazine from his M-16, and was holding it out to him.

"I thought the sergeant said-"

"Aw, fuck him. He shouldn't go around sneaking up on guys in the dark. Get yourself some sleep, cherry. I'll take the watch for awhile."

The ammo boxes were hard, his clothes damp and clammy; but these discomforts were no match for his overwhelming weariness. As Andy closed his eyes, he remembered the girl he had been with this afternoon. Lee was sweet and very beautiful, and she liked him, he could tell. A girl like that should not have been working in a place like the Houston Bar. He wondered if there might be some way that he could rescue her from that place, get her a job on one of the base camp work crews. Or perhaps he could even help her pay her living expenses. Here in Viet Nam, his extra $65 a month of combat pay was probably a fortune. These were the weighty thoughts that occupied the mind of PFC Andrew Cullen, as he sank into the welcoming arms of sleep.

49

V.   JUNGLE RULES

On the morning of the first day of August, the men of the First Battalion, Sixth Cavalry were assembled at the division's helicopter landing area, known as the "Golf Course." The area had been given its name upon the arrival of the division's advance party a year before, when the commanding general had insisted that it be cleared by hand, rather than by bulldozers, to preserve the grass that was growing there. He had said he wanted the finished product to look like a golf course, and the name had stuck.

They had been waiting here since 0630, which was the time scheduled for the airlift. It was now 0730, and there was as yet no sign of the CH-47 Chinooks that were to take them to LZ English. No one was surprised by the helicopters' lateness. This was, after all, the Army.

Enduring the cold drizzle with the other members of the Third Platoon, PFC Cullen was distinguishable only by the newness of his equipment. Like the others, he was wearing green cotton poplin fatigues, jungle boots with nylon uppers, a steel pot with a camouflage cover held in place by an elastic band into which he had tucked a plastic bottle of mosquito repellent. His web belt supported two full canteens with small bottles of water purification tablets taped to the caps, two ammo pouches, each holding three M-16 magazines inside and two fragmentation grenades secured by straps on the outside, a bayonet, and an entrenching tool. The belt was supported by suspenders which helped distribute the weight of the gear and provided other places to fasten equipment. Two field dressing pouches were attached to the shoulder straps, as well as two smoke grenades.

The Army had issued him a nylon rucksack with a lightweight metal frame. In this he had packed fifteen more magazines, each loaded with nineteen rounds rather than the maximum of twenty, a wad of rifle cleaning patches and LSA silicone lubricant, a poncho and liner, three extra pairs of socks, two C-ration meals, a package of heat tabs, basic toiletries, a carton of cigarettes, a can of foot powder, and a roll of all-purpose green tape. The cleaning rod for his M-16 was carried on the rifle itself, bent through the carrying handle and poked through the hole beneath the front sight.

With the exception of Horvath, who was happy to be escaping the first sergeant's control, the men were glum at the prospect of leaving the safety of base camp. Sprawled next to their field gear, they were smoking cigarettes and discussing the rumors surrounding their deployment. LZ English was the Cav's staging area for operations along the coast, and it was the general consensus that the coastal plain was preferable to the jungles near the Cambodian border, where main force NVA units were more likely to be encountered.

"Don't get me wrong," Horvath told the nervous Private Cullen, "you can get your ass blown away there. We got in a hell of a fight last year at a place called Bong Son. But most of the time, all you have to worry about is a few scruffy VC and boo-coo booby traps. The walking is easier, and most of the time you can see where you're going- unlike the jungle, where you're lucky if you can see twenty feet ahead a you."

Snake had been lying with his head cushioned on his rucksack. He was nursing a terrible hangover after his final night in base camp. Now he raised himself up on one elbow to contribute his two cents to the discussion.

"Booby traps are what you gotta worry about, cherry," he confirmed. "That's where most of our casualties will come from. The slopeheads living in the villes are all VC sympathizers. You won't see any a them motherfuckers stepping on the damn things."

"Godless heathen," Jason Ash piped up. "We will smite them with the edge of the sword!"

"Aw, shut up, Preacher," Snake growled. "All you ever want to do is go around 'smiting' folks. Why can't you just save your 'smiting' for Charlie? We took him to Sin City with us once," he told Andy. "He beat up one of the whores. He was in a back room with this ol' gal, and we heard shouting. We busted in on him and there he was bareass nekkid smiting the hell outta her with the buckle end of his belt. He ain't what you'd call the life a the party, our friend the Preacher here."

"More like the death of the party," Horvath put in.

"The only reason we put up with him," Snake continued, "is that he's the best shot in the battalion, maybe even the whole brigade. He comes from some place in the Ozarks where everybody marries their cousin and they live on squirrels and possum that they hunt with their rifles. Tell me, Preacher, what's the tastiest part of a possum?"

"Its big fat flappin' mouth!"

"Uh-oh, I think I got him pissed off. He'll get over it though, bein' as I'm from the squad's southern contingent. I'm from Texas, and Sar'nt Bird is from Kentucky, so we can get away with joshing him. Don't you try it, though, cherry, you bein' a Yankee and all."

"ALL RIGHT, SADDLE UP! HERE THEY COME!"

The platoon sergeant's roar put an abrupt end to the discussion. The men snatched up their gear, as the air was filled with the wutta-wutta-wutta of the approaching choppers. More than a dozen Chinooks came into view, ungainly flying buses that seemed too large to be held aloft by their churning rotors. As one of the machines descended in front of them, the blast from the downdraft was so fierce that men clutched their steel pots to keep them from blowing off. Ducking their heads instinctively, they passed beneath the whirling blades and headed for the loading ramp that had been lowered to receive them.

The Chinook could easily accommodate thirty fully-equipped grunts, and Andy's platoon boarded as a unit. Crewmen who looked like astronauts in their visored flight helmets directed the men to web cargo seats on both sides of the fuselage. When the ramp closed, the interior of the helicopter was bathed in semi-darkness. The noise of the engines increased, and crewmen took their places behind the M-60 machine guns mounted in the doors behind the cockpit. The entire aircraft vibrated like a Mixmaster. Squeezed in between Snake and Jason Ash, Andy felt a bit queasy. It was his first ride in a helicopter, and he was not at all sure he was enjoying the experience. The Preacher's lips were moving as they lifted off, but whatever he was saying was lost in the uproar. He appeared to be praying and, in this instance, Andy was with him a hundred percent.

*

53

The flight was short and uneventful. By the time the helicopter's big rubber wheels bumped on the tarmac of LZ English, Andy had decided that being a sky trooper was not all that bad. Once you got used to that kind of flying, it was no scarier than a carnival ride, and a tame one at that.

The loading ramp came down, and the men of Third Platoon disembarked amid a maelstrom of swirling red dust. It was one of those rare moments during the monsoon season when the clouds broke and the sun came shining through. They were standing on a plateau that had been stripped of almost all vegetation. To the west lay a range of blue-green mountains. Clusters of tents, sandbagged buildings and fortifications were spread over a wide area. Like the First Cav's base camp at An Khe, LZ English was surprisingly large. With its airstrip and helicopter landing facilities, it was a replica of Camp Radcliff, but incomplete, a work in progress.

Sergeant Roundtree formed the platoon up and marched them off toward the eastern perimeter. As they passed by a group of troopers from another company, Andy heard a shout.

"Hey, Jughead!"

Clarence Tyree came up behind him, caught him around the waist and hoisted him into the air as easily as if he were a child.

"Hey, man, how you doin'? It's great to see you!"

"It's good to see you too, Ty. How are they treating you in Delta Company?"

"Okay, Ah guess. Ah got a couple brothuhs looking out for me, you know what Ah'm sayin'?"

"Sure. But I'm your brother too, right?"

"You mah best bro', man, mah number one brothuh. Ah wish we could a stuck togethuh."

"Me too. Hey, have you heard anything about where we're going?"

"Dey calls it a 'search an' destroy mission.' We goin' search the VC villes, den we goin' destroy 'em."

"Destroy the villages, Ty? That doesn't sound right."

"Only tellin' you what Ah hear, man. Hey, Ah better get back to mah squad or mah honky squad leaduh 'll kick mah black ass. You take care a yo'se'f, y'heah?"

"You too, Ty. Keep your head down, man."

After his friend had departed, Horvath moved up alongside him in the column.

"'Jughead,' is it? Ha! That ain't bad!"

Andy cursed under his breath. He had been hoping that the nickname that dogged him through basic and AIT had not been overheard.

"You call me that again, Horvath, and I'll shoot you."

"Watch it, cherry. We don't joke about shooting people out here."

*

Alpha Company camped in an open area between an artillery battery and a fuel dump containing dozens of five hundred-gallon bladders of JP4 aviation fuel. Across the road was an ammo dump that looked as if it could supply the entire division for a year. The area had been occupied by transient infantry units before, and a lot of useful stuff had been left behind. As the men went about scrounging materials for the construction of temporary hooches, Jason Ash sidled up to Andy and suggested that they build one together.

"I knew the first time I saw you, brother, that you are one of God's people. The other men in this squad are all godless heathen, except for Rodriguez, and he's a Catholic, which is even worse. You and me oughtta stick together. Am I right or wrong?"

"Well, uh—"

There was something creepy about Ash, and Andy was uncomfortable with the idea of getting too close to him; but he could see no way of politely declining his suggestion. He was relieved when Horvath came to his rescue.

"Sorry, Preacher, but Cullen is buddying up with me. Since I'm the one who brought him into this outfit, I feel like I'm kinda responsible for him. I don't want you guys blaming me if he fucks up."

Ash gave Horvath a dark look, but he did not argue the point. He walked away without another word.

"Can't tell when the rain is gonna start again," Horvath said cheerfully. "We better get to work."

They snapped their ponchos together to make a canopy, which they stretched over a rectangular enclosure of 105-millimeter ammo boxes filled with dirt and surrounded by a shallow drainage trench. After their hooch was completed, they ate a cold C-ration meal and lit a heat tab to boil water in their canteen cups for coffee. Relaxing with their drinks, they smoked the stale cigarettes that came with the

55

rations.

"Except for going to Sin City with Snake," Andy said, "this is the first downtime I've had since I got here. It feels funny. I don't know what to do with myself."

"That's easy," Horvath told him. "Clean your rifle."

"But I already cleaned it before we left Radcliff."

"One thing you gotta learn, Andy, if you're gonna be a boonierat: You can't clean your rifle too often. The M-16 is a pretty good weapon, and it can put out a lot of firepower, but it's got a nasty habit of jamming on you at very inconvenient times. Lemme see your rifle."

Andy handed over his M-16. Horvath ejected the magazine and worked the loading handle to make sure the breech was clear. Taking out the disassembly pin, he broke the weapon open and removed the bolt assembly from the frame.

"Look here," he said, waving Andy closer. "You see these barrel locking lugs? There's carbon in here, even though this weapon's probably only been test fired a couple times. You want to use pipe cleaners to get in here and in the gas port. You probably don't have any pipe cleaners, right?"

Andy shook his head.

"That's okay, I got plenty. You can use mine until you can get some for yourself. Now, remember to check your extractor and spring every day. If they are worn or burred, get new ones ASAP. Ninety percent a your jams are gonna be caused by a shell casing getting stuck in the chamber. That's why we carry the cleaning rod outside, so we can have it handy to poke out stuck brass."

Horvath slid the bolt assembly back into its mount, snapped the rifle closed and handed it back to Andy.

"Get in the habit of cleaning this baby every chance you get. Treat her right, and she'll take good care a you."

Andy gazed down at the weapon in his hands. Although it would have been a stretch to call it beautiful, there was a cleanliness of line, a blend of form and function, that certainly could have been considered artistic. He was surprised by the stirring of a feeling which, if he had not known better, he might have identified as love.

*

That afternoon, Andy joined Horvath atop the earth berm that separated the fuel dump from the adjacent 155-millimeter howitzer battery. They watched the gun bunnies going about their business, swabbing out the tubes of their howitzers, carrying ammo to the gun pits, and filling and placing sandbags in the continual process of improving fortifications that went on in every military encampment. The guns were silent, and the work progressed at a desultory pace, with many of the men sitting around talking or dozing in the shade.

A volleyball net had been set up in the open space between the gun pits and the battery's fire direction center and command bunkers. New entertainment was provided when several brawny enlisted men gathered on the court and started a game. Their enthusiasm was greater than their skill, and after observing them for awhile, Horvath concluded:

"We can kick their ass."

Returning to their camp, they found Sergeant Lawler inspecting his ammo and reloading his magazines.

"Hey Bird," Horvath said, "the cannoncockers next door are playing v-ball. What do you say we challenge them to a game?"

"What have they got that we want?"

"How about some hot chow? Those guys have their own mess hall. A hot meal would sure beat the hell outta the C's we're eating now."

"Sounds good to me. What about you, Cullen- ever play any volleyball?"

Andy had in fact played on an intramural team in college, and had found that his basketball skills were well suited to the game. Remembering Horvath's warning about disclosing his college background, however, he decided to keep this information close to his chest.

"Sure, I've played some."

"Great! Welcome to the team. You guys go ahead and get the game set up. I'll round up Snake and Hot Rod, and we'll be along in a couple minutes."

"Roger that, sarge."

As they descended the berm and approached the game in progress, Horvath spoke to Andy from the side of his mouth:

"Let me do the talking, okay?"

When a break occurred in the action, Horvath approached a squat fireplug of a man who looked somewhat older than the others, and therefore was probably in a position of authority.

"Hey there, sarge," he said. "We're from A-1-6, camped next door. We were wondering if you guys would like a little competition."

The man did not correct Horvath's assumption as to his rank.

"Sure," he said, "why not?"

"I gotta warn you, though," Horvath added, "we're pretty damn good."

The challenge was delivered with just the right mixture of arrogance and good humor, and Andy had the distinct impression that Horvath had played this role before. The glint in the artillery sergeant's eye indicated that he was rising to the bait.

"Is that so?"

"Hey, why don't we make it interesting? Say the losing team treats the winners to chow?"

"Ha! You gotta be kidding! I just happen to be the mess sergeant of this battery, and our menu for supper is spaghetti with meat sauce. What would I be getting from you if I win?"

"We got C-rats, sarge. I think mine is ham and lima beans."

The artillery sergeant snorted derisively.

"Look, we can play for fun if you want, but you can keep your ham and motherfuckers. Nice try, private."

Horvath appeared crestfallen at this response. With a show of great reluctance, he dug into the pocket of his trousers and pulled out a swatch of colored material, which he unfolded and held up for inspection. Andy recognized the red and blue rectangles with the gold star of the Viet Cong flag. Even a new guy knew that this was the most prized of all the Nam's souvenirs.

Now it was the sergeant who was trying to disguise his eagerness; but his eyes, darting repeatedly to the flag, burned with avarice.

"Where did you get that, private?"

"I personally took it off a Cong KIA in Happy Valley."

"And you're willing to play for it?"

"Well, I think this is worth more than a meal for just a squad. How about supper for our whole platoon if we win?"

"One game?"

"One game."

"Jungle rules?"

"Sure, what else?"

"All right, private, you're on. Go ahead and get your team."

"Actually, sarge, I see them coming now."

Bird Lawler and Snake Holloway were coming over the berm, with Pete Rodriguez walking between them. They were both several inches over six feet, and Hot Rod's diminutive size served to emphasize their height. The artillery sergeant's eyes narrowed shrewdly.

"Doggone me, I believe I been hustled. Ciccone!" he snapped, and one of the gun bunnies jumped to attention. "Go and get Lurtsema. Tell him we need him on the volleyball court ASAP."

"I think Lurch is asleep, sarge," Ciccone protested. "He was up all night humpin' ammo. I don't want to bother him when he's sleeping."

"Just do it, goddamnit!"

The man looked as if he had been given an order to charge a machine gun, but he clamped his mouth shut and departed. The sergeant picked the volleyball up from the ground and tossed it to Horvath.

"Why don't you boys warm up?" he said. "We'll be ready to rock 'n roll in a couple of minutes."

As Third Squad batted the ball around, Andy realized that one of their members was missing, a fact upon which he remarked to Snake Holloway.

"Preacher don't play games," Snake replied. "He thinks they're the devil's work."

Word of the match apparently had spread, for men were drifting over from the gun pits and forming a circle around the court, and a growing number of A-1-6 troopers were lining the top of the berm. Andy could not be certain, but he thought he saw the Preacher's white-blond head among them. An excited murmur rose, and the crowd parted to admit a gangly, lantern-jawed individual dressed only in underwear and unlaced combat boots, who did in fact bear a striking resemblance to the Addams Family butler.

"My God," Hot Rod breathed, "he must be seven feet tall."

"Don't worry," Snake scoffed. "That thing don't look like it can tie its shoes, much less hit a volleyball."

Andy had to agree. As he stood knock-kneed, blinking in the sunlight and scratching the crotch of his baggy shorts, the giant did not look like much of a threat.

"Volley for serve!"

After the ball had been batted back and forth a few token times, play began in earnest. Third Squad's teamwork was immediately apparent, as Horvath bumped the ball to Hot Rod, who popped up a perfect set that was then cleanly spiked by Snake. The serve was theirs.

Horvath launched a low arcing overhand serve. As the ball cleared the net, a long sinewy arm reached up nonchalantly and batted it to the ground. It happened so suddenly, it took Third Squad a moment to register what had occurred.

"Did you see that?" Hot Rod exclaimed. "He didn't even jump!"

"You can't spike the serve," Andy protested. "It's not legal."

"We're playing jungle rules," said Horvath. "In jungle rules, it's legal."

"It was an accident," grumbled Bird, "just pure dumb luck."

He could not have been more wrong. With Lurch staggering around and flailing his arms in a fashion that appeared spastic but was actually devastatingly effective, the artillerymen reeled off seven straight points. To their credit, though, the men of Third Squad did not quit. They hung on grimly, scrapping for every ball as if their very lives were at stake, until Hot Rod's diving scoop was followed by a lucky shot by Bird that struck the top of the net and dribbled over, winning them back the serve.

The weaknesses of their opponents were now exposed, as Bird lofted one high serve after another, drawing a series of comedic errors that provoked groans from the cannoncockers and laughter and rude remarks from the troopers atop the berm. The streak extended for five points before the mess sergeant succeeded in bumping up a set that Lurch smashed to the earth.

In possession of the serve again, the artillerymen resumed their scoring, with Lurch pounding down every ball that came anywhere near him. The score was 12-5, and the situation looked bleak, when Andy fooled the big man by faking a spike and popping the ball gently over his head. The top of the berm erupted in cheering, and Andy was surprised to hear his own name being called by the crowd. It had been a long time since he had experienced this, and he was amazed at how good it felt. As he moved back to serve, he was pumped up with an adrenaline rush. Unfortunately, his excitement got the better of him. He hit the serve too hard, and the ball carried far beyond the end line of the court. A collective sigh escaped the crowd.

Now Lurch rotated back to the serving position. He launched a bullet, which Hot Rod dove to retrieve and somehow managed to keep in play. Bird got his hands on the ball in what would have been considered a carry under strict rules, and flipped it over to Horvath, who drove a well-aimed shot to the far corner. Side out, and Snake took the ball.

Snake proved to be an effective server, changing speeds and finding locations like a big league pitcher. And with Lurch now on the back line, it had become a whole different ball game at the net. The men of Third Squad began clawing their way back into the game. They won four consecutive points, five, six. The score stood 12-11 when Snake finally lost the serve by grazing the top of the net.

The cannoncockers scored two more points, one on a service winner, and the next when Bird's cross-court spike was called wide, a questionable call that brought howls from the infantrymen and their supporters. A near riot ensued, and the intervention of two officers from the artillery battery was necessary to restore order. Third Squad was now on the brink of extinction. It is time, as they said in the military vernacular, to "do or die."

The serve came to Andy, and as he bumped it, he moved forward in a classic "give and go." Understanding his intention, Bird popped up a perfect set. As he leapt upward, Andy saw from his peripheral vision that Lurch was charging the net. The scene took on a dreamlike quality, with everything happening in slow motion: the ball floating through the air, himself rising to reach it, and the big man bearing down on him on a collision course. Certain that he could make the play, he cocked his arm, preparing to unleash a powerful spike.

The ball seemed literally to explode in his face, driving him backwards into the dirt. Stunned, he touched his fingers to the blood streaming from his nose, as the chants of the crowd rang in his ears.

"Lurch! Lurch! Lurch!"

It was not fair. The ball plainly had been on his side of the net. Through pain-clouded eyes he saw the big man towering far above him, extending a hand to help him up.

"Sorry about that, buddy. Jungle rules."

*

Someone had scrounged a case of beer, and the celebration in the bivouac area was becoming spirited. The encounter with the artillerymen had been the stuff of which folklore was made, and already the members of Third Squad were embellishing the truth. Anyone listening would have thought they had won a glorious victory, rather than suffering an ignominious defeat.

"Did you see the way Hot Rod kept making those digs? Anything within ten feet of him stayed up. It was amazing, man!"

"What about Snake's serve? He had those cannoncockers falling all over each other. Nothing but smoke!"

"The play I liked best was when the cherry dinked the ball over that big gorilla. Man, did he look stupid!"

The praise was music to Andy's ears. They were actually treating him like one of them. He knocked back the last of his second beer, and another was immediately put in his hand.

"Did you see the look on that sergeant's face," Horvath chortled, "when I put that rag in his hand? He thought he had himself a genuine VC flag."

"It wasn't a real flag?" Andy asked in surprise.

"Hell no! I bought that thing for a buck at the Special Forces camp in Happy Valley. The montagnard strikers' wives were turning 'em out by the hundreds."

The flag was worthless, and the game had been a can't-lose proposition from the start. Andy realized that maybe they really had won after all.

"Geez," he said, there's more to this 'jungle rules' stuff than meets the eye."

*

"DROP YOUR SOCKS AND GRAB YOUR COCKS! LET'SGOLET'SGOLET'SGO!"

As if rising from the darkest depths of the ocean, Andy struggled up toward consciousness. When he had lain down and rolled himself up in his poncho liner the night before, relaxed in a pleasant glow of alcohol and friendship, he had been anticipating a long and restful sleep. No sooner had he closed his eyes, however, than- BOOM!— the night had been shattered by a tremendous explosion that sounded as if it had come right next to his hooch. His first thought had been that they were being mortared. He had been thrashing about wildly, trying to disentangle himself from the poncho liner, when Horvath had told him to calm down.

"It's just the artillery," he had explained, "shooting H and I's."

"What the hell is that?"

"'Harassment and interdiction.' They shoot all night at targets like stream crossings and trail junctions. It gives Charlie something to think about when he's snooping and pooping around out there."

"They keep shooting all night?"

"About every fifteen minutes or so. Don't worry, you get used to it. After awhile, you get so you can sleep through anything."

As if to prove his point, Horvath had rolled over and within seconds had been snoring. Andy had lain awake, anticipating the next explosion. Sure enough, in exactly fifteen minutes, another mighty blast had shaken the ground and set his ears ringing. What lunacy, he had thought. He was the one being harassed, not Charlie.

It had been after midnight when he had finally drifted off. Then the rain had come, falling in torrents that had overwhelmed the capacity of the shallow drainage trench that he and Horvath had dug around their hooch. Cold water had come seeping in beneath the wall of ammo boxes, and soon the side of him that was in contact with the ground had been soaked. He remembered Horvath advising him to bring along a second poncho, a suggestion that he had rejected because he had not wanted to carry the extra weight. Horvath had not explained his reasoning at the time. Now, as Horvath used his extra poncho as a ground sheet, an explanation was no longer necessary.

In spite of the noise and discomfort, sheer exhaustion finally had caused him to lapse into unconsciousness. Seemingly only minutes later, he was hearing the sounds of an infantry company coming awake: groans and farts, belches and curses, the clink of canteen cups and the snick-thwack of rifle bolts.

Rolling over and throwing off his poncho liner, he got up onto his hands and knees and crawled out into the gray daylight. The rain had let up. Only a light drizzle fell upon his upturned face. His joints creaked and his muscles protested, as he rose unsteadily to his feet. After all the beer he had drunk the night before, his bladder felt as if it were about to burst. Unbuttoning his trousers, he relieved himself where he stood.

Horvath was kneeling with a steel mirror in one hand and a safety razor in the other. Tendrils of steam were rising from the shell of his helmet resting upside down on the ground in front of him. A cheerful grin split the lather covering his face.

"G' morning, sunshine. I got hot water for shaving from the artillery mess hall. I'll let you have some, if you make the coffee."

That sounded like a fair deal to Andy. He used one of his heat tabs to get water boiling in his canteen cup and dumped in packets of instant coffee and sugar. He and Horvath breakfasted on C-ration fruit and crackers with plastic cheese, then had a cigarette with their coffee. In their rough and uncomfortable surroundings, the hot sweet drink and the tobacco seemed incredible luxuries.

"So, what'll we do today," said Andy, blowing a plume of smoke, "challenge the cannoncockers again?"

"Hell no," Horvath replied. "The platoon sergeant came by before you woke up and told us to get our shit together. It looks like you're going to get your feet wet, cherry. We're going on an air assault this morning."

VI. SHORT-TIMER'S DISEASE

As he waits on the tarmac for the Hueys that will take them away from LZ English, Andy's limbs are afflicted by a numbing paralysis, and his bowels feel as if they have turned to water. He wonders if his fear shows, if the others can see that they have a coward in their midst. Their own faces reveal little of what they are thinking. They appear pretty much as usual: Bird calm and composed; Horvath cheerfully alert; Hot Rod scowling, his eyes glowing with suppressed anger; Preacher as serene as a martyr going to the stake. Only Snake looks a little bit peaked, paler than usual, with a muscle twitching in his jaw.

They have no idea where they are going. Horvath has told Andy that there is nothing unusual about that.

"They never tell us nothing. To them we're just pawns on a checkerboard."

Horvath also told him not to worry.

"Just stick with me, Andy. Watch me and do what I do. Remember Charlie's tracers are green, or sometimes white. If you see green tracers, you'll know the LZ is hot."

"What do I do then?"

"Keep your ass down and take cover. Stick with me, and you'll be okay."

Over by the perimeter, the artillery battery starts firing; not just an occasional round, as during the night, but a steady barrage with all of the howitzers shooting together.

"That'll be our LZ prep," Horvath explains. SOP is the arty pounds the landing zone to soften it up just before we come in. That means the choppers are on the way."

Somewhere down the line, a voice is raised, whining out the lyrics of an old familiar tune.

"Please, Mr. Custer, Ah don' wanna go-o-o-o!"

Andy sees the Hueys coming, lots of them, filling the sky like a swarm of monstrous dragonflies. The UH1-D troop carriers are called "slicks," with no weaponry except for the M-60 machine guns mounted on either side. As they come swooping in by two's, the noise of their turbine engines rises to a deafening roar.

The men of Third Squad sprint toward the third chopper on their side of the pickup zone. Moving awkwardly under his sixty-pound load, Andy lags a bit, but he keeps Horvath's broad back squarely in focus. Before he can reach the chopper, however, two men suddenly cut in between him and Horvath. Recognizing Sergeant Roundtree, the acting platoon leader, and his RTO, he stands back deferentially to let them climb aboard. When he steps forward, a door gunner who does not look a day older than fifteen waves him off.

"We're over our load limit," he screams. "We've already got one too many!"

Andy freezes for a moment; then he realizes what he must do. As fast as he can, he runs back to the next Huey in line. That, too, is full. He runs back to another. No dice. He is caught in a nightmare game of musical chairs from which there seems to be no escape. Coming to the next chopper, he ignores the door gunner's hand waving and throws himself aboard just as it is lifting off.

His relief at finding a place quickly evaporates, as the nose of the helicopter tilts forward and it gathers speed. The cargo bay is without seats or accommodations of any kind, and he is lying facedown on a bare metal floor studded with rivets. When the ship banks to turn eastward, he begins sliding toward the open doorway. Like most sane people, Andy has always been afraid of heights. As he looks over his shoulder at the widening gulf between the helicopter and the ground, his fear escalates to terror. He does the only thing that he can do under the circumstances. Seeing nothing else to hang on to, he grasps the ankle of the man next to him.

It is an awkward moment, made worse by the fact that he does not know the person he has just grabbed. He looks up from the jungle boot that he is hanging onto for dear life into the face of a stranger, a trooper no older than himself. His face is stiff and expressionless, and Andy realizes that this boy is every bit as scared as he is. Somehow that makes the situation a little bit better.

When they have leveled off at a thousand feet, Andy feels secure enough to shift his position. He lets go of the trooper's ankle and sits in front of the open doorway with his knees pulled up to his chest. They are flying toward the South China Sea along a valley rimmed on either side with mountains. He sees below them the geometric patterns of rice paddies, an occasional village and a road clogged with people, presumably refugees. At the far end of the valley, a ridge juts out onto the plain. Near its base, orange flashes are blossoming amid a pall of dark brown smoke. He realizes that what he is seeing must be the artillery prep pounding the landing zone. In another minute they have drawn even with the landing zone. As they pass by to the north, the orange flashes cease, and he sees a column of white smoke rising into the sky. At some point along the way they have acquired an escort of ARA gunships, armed Hueys bristling with rockets. One of the gunships is flying alongside them, so close he can see the grim faces of the pilots and crew.

Wheeling left, they make a roller coaster descent to treetop level and come screaming into the LZ at ninety miles an hour. The door gunners are firing continuously, and rockets are streaking from the gunships. In spite of his fear, Andy experiences a rush of exhilaration at the awesome display of the Cav's firepower. He sees no tracers, green or otherwise, but amid all the noise and smoke it is impossible to tell for sure whether or not they are being shot at.

The slick in which he is riding brakes sharply, flaring its nose. The "clearing" below him turns out to be covered with tall grass that ripples like water under the rotor's downdraft. The pilot does not land, but brings the ship to a hover with its belly almost touching the tops of the grass. The door gunner screams in his ear.

"Jump!"

This was not what he expected, but there is no time to discuss the matter. He braces his feet on the skid. *Fuck it*, he thinks, and launches himself into space. He comes down hard, but intact, and the weight of his gear throws him to his knees. The helicopters have departed, and all is quiet. The valley reacts with stunned silence to the thunderous arrival of Alpha Company, First Battalion of the Sixth Cavalry Regiment.

He is amazed by the denseness of the grass, which rises above his head and presses in on him from all sides. Hearing someone thrash by a few feet away, he moves over and follows the trail that has been beaten through the grass. Every few feet, he passes a long, sharpened bamboo stake stuck in the ground. The enemy knew that the area might be used as a landing zone, and prepared it accordingly. His testicles retract, as he realizes what the result of his jump might have been, had he not been lucky.

Presently the grass thins, and the ground slopes upward. He comes upon several members of the Weapons Platoon, Danielson, the hapless helicopter mechanic, among them, setting up a mortar tube. He asks them if they know where he might find the Third Platoon, and a sergeant tells him to look in the six-to-nine o'clock sector. He remembers Horvath saying that the company used a "clock" system in securing a landing zone, but, as he was planning on staying close to his mentor, he did not bother to learn where his own platoon's area of responsibility would be. He resolves not to make that mistake again.

*

Andy is reunited with the Third Squad, when he literally stumbles over Pete Rodriguez. With tufts of grass adorning his helmet and rucksack, Hot Rod is almost invisible in the depression where he is lying.

"Where the hell have you been, cherry?" he snarls. "Get your ass down before somebody shoots it off for you."

He hunkers down and brings his rifle to his shoulder, sighting down the barrel and trying to look alert. He can see no more than a few feet ahead of him, as clumps of broad-leafed vegetation effectively block his vision.

"What are we doing?" he whispers. "What's going on?"

Yesterday he and the Mexican from Los Angeles were teammates and drinking buddies. Hot Rod told him his life story, from his childhood in the *barrio* right up to the time a judge gave him a choice between going to jail for participating in a gang fight and enlisting in the Army. Today, it is as if none of it ever happened.

"Shut up," Hot Rod tells him.

Stung, he zips his mouth shut and waits for someone to tell him what to do. He does not have to wait long. Sergeant Roundtree strolls by (apparently no one told him to get his ass down) and tells them to move out in single file to the north. All around him, the men of the Third Platoon rise up and melt into the bushes. Seeing the platoon sergeant and his RTO joining the middle of the column, he moves to follow them.

A hand falls on his arm, holding him back. He turns, startled, and sees that it is Horvath who has appeared seemingly out of no-where.

"Wait," Horvath says softly. "Never walk behind a radio opera-tor if you can help it. Charlie knows that only officers and noncoms have radios, so anyone near an RTO is a target. Fall in behind me. Try to stay at least five paces back, but don't let me get out of sight. Sorry about losing you on the airlift. When the platoon sergeant jumped into our stick, I couldn't do anything about it. See you later, okay?"

Horvath grins and gives his arm a squeeze before trotting off to join the column. As instructed, Andy follows several paces behind him.

Emerging from the bushes, they are confronted by an expanse of flooded rice paddies. Green shoots poke up through the surface of the brown water, which is dimpled by falling rain. Black clouds are rolling in from the east, threatening a greater downpour. A Company sets out across the paddies, with First and Second Platoons covering the flanks, Third Platoon lagging somewhat behind them at the center, and the Weapons Platoon bringing up the rear.

The paddies are segmented by narrow earthen dikes, the tops of which barely protrude above the water. The platoons move in single file, picking their way along the dikes. They are out in the open, easy targets for anyone who might be lurking in the distant tree line. Imag-ining an unseen rifleman drawing a bead on him, Andy feels extremely uneasy. He wishes that he were wearing the flak vest that he was issued; but none of the men wear them, as they are considered too hot and heavy for the field.

Andy's nervousness leads to clumsiness. He slips on the muddy ground, and before he can recover, loses his balance and slides off the dike. He manages to remain upright as he lands in the shallow water, but quickly sinks up to his knees in clinging muck. Struggling to free himself, he sinks even deeper. He is beginning to panic, when he sees Horvath bending over him, extending a hand.

"Happens to everyone," Horvath says with a grin. "Don't sweat it."

There is a wet, sucking sound, as Andy is pulled from the muck. Standing on the dike again, he looks down at his pants and sees that they are coated with brown slime. The smell is foul, and he recalls hearing that the Vietnamese fertilize their rice crop with human shit.

He notices something else, two slug-like creatures clinging to his trouser leg. With a shudder of revulsion, he realizes what they are.

"Better get rid of those leeches," Horvath tells him. "Once they get attached, it's a lot harder to get them off."

Reaching down, he brushes the clammy things off him.

"Hey," a voice calls, "what's going on back there?"

He realizes, to his great embarrassment, that he has been holding up the entire column.

"It's okay," Horvath replies. "Move 'em out."

The rain continues, gray sheets sweeping across the paddies. Although soaked to the skin, Andy is not uncomfortable, as the exertion of the march keeps him warm. The rain also serves to rinse the muck from his trousers. As it becomes clear that he is not in imminent danger, his nervousness begins to fade, and he begins almost to enjoy himself.

"Hey," Hot Rod calls, "any a you guys heard a somebody called Wayne Morse?"

He has picked up a slip of paper that was lying on the paddy dike and is holding it up for inspection.

"It says here the guy is a U.S. senator. It says that he says the war is wrong, and 'just because we're mighty, we don't have the right to try to substitute might for right.' He says, 'America is the greatest threat to the peace of the world.' Now, how do you like that?"

"Get rid of that," Bird tells him. "It's bullshit. There ain't no 'Wayne Morse,' and if there is, he never said nothing like that. Psy ops is all it is. Charlie is trying to fuck with our minds."

Andy could have set him straight, but he is keeping a low profile when it comes to showing what he knows. He walks on in silence, taking in a scene that is a landscape painter's fantasy. Softened by the mist and rain, the emerald green valley is cupped like a jewel amid the darker green of the surrounding mountains. Off to the northeast, perhaps a kilometer away, a farmer in a conical hat is working with a buffalo in a rice paddy. He cannot make out exactly what the man is doing, but can see that his trousers are rolled above his knees as he follows some sort of implement, a plow, perhaps, that the beast is pulling through the muck. Amazing, he thinks, the guy is going about his usual business in the middle of a war.

KAPOW-W-W-w-w-w-w!

A single shot echoes across the open space of the paddies. Andy ducks and freezes in place. Turning, he sees Specialist Jason Ash holding his rifle in the classic kneeling position, right elbow jutting parallel to the ground, left arm extended and braced on his knee, the wood stock of the weapon snug against his cheek. The Preacher is the only member of the Third Platoon who carries an M-14, the enhanced version of the old M-1 Garand. Chambered for the 7.62 millimeter NATO cartridge, the M-14 is considerably heavier than the M-16, but it also has a greater effective range.

Seeing the direction in which the Preacher's barrel is pointing, he gets a sinking feeling. He looks out across the paddies, and the farmer has disappeared. The buffalo is standing still, craning its neck about as if confused. Andy goes numb, his brain refusing to accept what his eyes are telling him.

"You missed him, Preacher," Snake says.

"The heck I did," Ash retorts, his pale eyes glittering like ice. "It was a perfect head shot."

Andy is sickened. He wants desperately to believe that Snake is right, and that the Viet farmer is now hiding behind a paddy dike; but Ash's voice had a ring of certainty.

The platoon sergeant's radio crackles, and the voice of Captain Roth, the company commander, can be heard on the speaker asking what the shooting was about.

"Not incoming," Sergeant Roundtree replies. "Just one of the men getting trigger-happy."

"Maintain fire discipline," the captain tells him. "Six out."

"Knock it off back there!" the platoon sergeant shouts. "Fire only when fired upon. You want to tell the whole world where we are?"

It occurs to Andy that arriving by helicopter after an artillery barrage and marching in company strength across the open paddies might at least give Charlie a hint as to their location. What is really troubling, though, is the shooting of an innocent civilian. He cannot believe that such a thing would be condoned, and he decides that Sergeant Roundtree must not have noticed the farmer. As the platoon continues to march, he considers whether he ought to report what he has seen. He did not actually see the farmer fall, and it is possible that the man is still alive; but in his heart, he knows that not to be so. He decides to seek Horvath's advice on the matter at the earliest opportunity.

Leaving the paddies behind, they cross a crude wooden bridge spanning a drainage ditch and stop at the edge of a clearing. On the other side of the clearing is a bamboo hedge row, beyond which can be seen the tousled tops of palm trees and the thatched roofs of a village.

Sergeant Roundtree spreads his arms in a signal for the platoon to go on line. Andy takes a position a few yards from Horvath, crouching down behind a bush which, although not providing much in the way of cover, at least offers some concealment. Without a single good night's sleep since arriving in-country, he has been operating on adrenaline. Now that he feels safe, at least for the moment, his exhaustion catches up with him. Seeing that others around him are taking advantage of the break in the march to relax a bit, he removes his steel pot and slips out of the straps of his rucksack. Tired and with aching muscles, he realizes that he is also terribly thirsty. His anxiety has been so great, it has not occurred to him to take a drink since leaving LZ English. Opening one of the two one-quart plastic canteens that he carries, he raises it to his lips. The water is warm, but it tastes like nectar of the gods.

CRACK! CRACK! CRACK! CRACK! CRACK!

The sound of an AK-47 firing at him from close range is unlike anything he has ever imagined. It is the sound of the end of the world. He reacts instinctively, writhing, rolling, somehow keeping moving until there is no ground under him and he drops to safety. Sobbing for breath, he stares up at the leaden sky, as water at the bottom of the drainage ditch soaks through the back of his fatigues. He hears shouts, and the staccato popping of M-16's, as the men of Alpha Company begin to return the enemy fire.

Through a series of contortions, he manages to get himself upright in the ditch and peers cautiously over the edge. In AIT you were taught that if you were caught in an ambush, you let out a yell- aaargh!- and charged in the direction of the enemy, firing your weapon from the hip. This is not what the members of the Third Platoon have done. All the men he can see are sprawled upon the ground, whether living or dead he cannot tell. Somewhat belatedly, he remembers that his job in this situation is to be a rifleman. Although he has no recollection of picking it up, his M-16 is in his hands. Emptying his magazine toward the bamboo thicket in one long burst, he yells at the top of his lungs.

"Over here!"

His shout is swallowed up by the horrendous uproar. As he reloads his weapon, he realizes that his pack and helmet, as well as one of his canteens, are still lying beside the bush ten meters away. Those ten meters might as well be ten miles, for all practical purposes, for there is nothing in the world that would make him leave the ditch. He has only the six magazines that he carries in his ammo pouches. Moving the selector switch of his rifle to the single-shot position, he searches for a target. There is no sign of the enemy, and he is beginning to wonder if they are still receiving fire, when he hears a whack like a bat striking a baseball, and a neat hole appears in the tree behind his head.

Terrified, he ducks down, as the noise of the firefight gathers and swells, the various weapons of the infantry company joining in a symphonic crescendo. The pop-pop-pop of the M-16's is punctuated by the ka-powwws of the Preacher's M-14 and backed up by the jackhammer pounding of an M-60 machine gun. Poink?... poink?... poink? queries a nearby M-79 grenade launcher. Other troopers are taking cover in the ditch, tumbling in on either side of him. When he finds the nerve to raise his head and peek out again, he sees Horvath sliding towards him like a baseball player stealing home. Coming after him are Bird Lawler and PFC Raul Martinez, the platoon's RTO, running hunched over, dragging the prostrate form of Sergeant Roundtree by the arms.

They all flop in on top of him, landing in a heap of arms and legs and equipment. When they untangle themselves from one another, it becomes apparent that the platoon sergeant is badly hurt. His lips are drawn back from his teeth in a snarl of anguish, and his brown face has turned a sickly shade of gray. A crimson stain is widening on his right leg, just above the knee.

Horvath tears away the wounded man's trouser leg, exposing a dark puncture from which blood continues to well.

"Turn over on your side, sarge," he says. "I want to have a look at the exit wound."

Bird has the radio handset and is trying to contact the company commander.

"Diamondback Six, Diamondback Six, this is Three-Six Alpha, over."

When he releases the transmit button, even though the speaker is not turned on, Andy is close enough to hear the babble of voices vying for space on the company net. First Platoon has overrun an ambush position and is reporting three enemy KIA's. The Weapons Platoon is maneuvering to reinforce the center of the line.

"...Doesn't look too bad, sarge," Horvath is saying. "How does it feel?"

"It hurts like hell," Sergeant Roundtree answers through clenched teeth.

"That's a good sign. If it was really bad, you wouldn't be feeling any pain. Hey, Andy, let me have one of your field dressings."

On one side of Andy, Jason Ash has his elbows braced on the edge of the trench and is firing well-spaced shots, his torso jerking with the recoil of his weapon. On the other side, Snake Holloway is raising his M-16 above his head and sending unaimed bursts in the general direction of the enemy. As Snake's approach appears much the safer, this is the one that Andy decides to adopt. Keeping his head down, he pokes the barrel of his rifle over the edge of the dirt and squeezes off a round.

"…Diamondback Three-Six is hit," Bird is saying. He has finally succeeded in getting through to Captain Roth. "I say again, Three-Six is down. Request instructions, over."

Sergeant Lawler listens intently to what the captain is saying.

"Roger that," he says. He puts down the handset, his expression greatly relieved.

"Cap'n says to stay put. The FO is calling in arty."

The words have hardly left his lips, when a fluttering whine can be heard above the sounds of small arms fire that culminates in a POP! and red smoke streamers arch in above the palm trees.

"Right on the money!" Bird shouts. "HE is on the way. Get down!"

All along the ditch, the troopers duck and cover. Andy pictures in his mind the cannoncockers on LZ English scrambling to load the heavy projectiles, the shouted commands as the firing data is cranked into the big guns. Less than twenty-four hours ago, he was playing volleyball with those guys.

s-h-h-h-e-e-e-e-e-E-E-E-EE…

With the sound of a rushing freight train, the artillery volley arrives. The ground lurches, and the air is shattered with the force of six high explosive rounds exploding simultaneously.

CRUMP! RUMPH-WHUMP! CA-RUMP!

The sledgehammer concussions have an immediate and dramatic effect on the firefight. Both sides stop shooting, as they digest the implications of what has just occurred. Horvath slides up close to Andy to speak directly in his ear.

"Charlie ain't gonna just sit there and let us chew him up. He'll either assault us now or disengage. My guess is he'll dee-dee, but keep your eyes open."

Andy ventures a peek into no-man's land. Beyond the bamboo hedge, a pall of smoke hangs over the village. Trees have been snapped like matchsticks, their jagged stumps jutting up like giant punji stakes.

"Get down!" Bird screams. "Battery three on the way!"

The effect of each of the battery's six howitzers firing three rounds in quick succession is nothing short of staggering. The men of Alpha Company cower in the ditch, as the earth erupts less than a hundred yards away in a maelstrom of smoke and fire and flying steel. The flash-CRACK! Of a tree burst sends shrapnel screaming overhead. Then all is quiet again, save for the snap, crackle and pop of burning bamboo, and an occasional splat and hiss, as a piece of spent shrapnel falls into the ditch. A weak cheer rises along the ditch.

"That's the way it works, Andy," says Horvath. "Most of the time we're just out here for target acquisition. We're dangled out here like bait, and when Charlie bites, we call in a lot of firepower and blow the shit out of him. Now you know what it feels like, being a worm wriggling on a hook."

Bird Lawler is listening intently to a message coming over the company net. He nods, and then gives the handset back to his RTO.

"It's over, guys," he says. "Pass the word: we're pulling back."

*

Night has fallen. Alpha Company has set up a defensive perimeter on a finger of high ground on the outskirts of the village. Sergeant Roundtree having been medevaced, command of Third Platoon has been turned over to Second Lieutenant Arthur ("Dingle") Berry, formerly the leader of the Weapons Platoon. Dingle Berry is small and rodent-faced, with a pursed mouth dominated by a set of oversized choppers and framed by a weedy mustache. His mouth, Snake Holloway remarked, "looks like an asshole with teeth." It is the general consensus of the men that the arrival of Lt. Berry on the scene is not a positive development.

Andy has retrieved his saddle-up gear from no-man's land at the time of the pullback. His pack has been riddled by shrapnel, one of his canteens is ruined, and there is a bullet hole drilled through the exact center of his helmet. He and Anton Horvath are sharing a foxhole overlooking the rice paddies that they crossed earlier in the day. Horvath insisted that they dig the hole, even though many of the members of their platoon have opted for less secure arrangements.

"I'm responsible for you," he said, "and it's my job to see that you get in the right habits. It don't matter how tired you are- always dig a hole, and make it the best hole you can. Maybe not tonight, maybe not tomorrow night, but some night you're gonna be glad you got that hole, I guaran-fucking-tee it."

The ground here is soft, and the hole that they have dug is a good one, six feet long and five feet deep, with a shelf at the bottom. The two troopers are, at present, sitting on the shelf at the bottom of the hole, enjoying the luxury of a cigarette.

"I guess," Andy is saying, "I'm not a cherry anymore."

"Guess again, buddy. You're still a cherry."

"But I've been in combat now."

"That wasn't combat; that was just a little skirmish. I'll say this for you, though, you did pretty good. I never saw anyone move as fast as you did when that AK-47 opened up. You were in that ditch before any of us. One thing I noticed, though: You were firing your weapon without aiming it. You gotta see what you're shooting at to be effective. They taught you that in basic, right?"

"Yeah, I guess so. But Snake was firing blind. I was just copying him."

"Snake is a good soldier, but right now he's got a problem. We call it 'short-timer's disease.' When you first get here, Andy, it's scary as hell. You see guys getting zapped, and you know it can happen to you. You either drive yourself nuts worrying about it, or you toughen up. You let go of the idea of staying alive, and you get on with it. But when you last out almost a whole year, you can't help thinking, hey, I just might make it back to the Land of the Big PX. And then you start getting scared all over again."

"So I'm a dead duck, that's what you're telling me?"

"No way! You got a chance to make it through this, and you can make your odds better by getting your shit together. But I am telling you not to think too much about making it back home. It'll only make you crazy. A couple days ago, I heard Snake asking Sergeant Roundtree if he could stay in base camp when the rest of us went out to the boonies. He was begging him, man, he was pleading. The sarge told him he had to come, that we needed every man. I am telling you that Snake may not the best one to be patterning yourself after, right now."

"I can buy that, Anton. Hey, thanks, man."

"No sweat, buddy. We'll make a boonierat outta you yet."

Andy considers bringing up the topic of the farmer who was gunned down in the paddies in the afternoon; but somehow, after everything that has happened, it no longer seems to be such a big deal. Reminding himself that he did not actually see anything, he decides to let the matter drop, at least for now.

*

He is awakened in darkness by a hand shaking his shoulder. He does not remember trying to fall asleep, is amazed to have done so soaking wet, sitting upright at the bottom of a hole.

"Hey," Horvath says, "how you doing, man?"

"Not too bad," he replies, realizing as he says this that it is true. Although nowhere near enough to get rid of his deep weariness, a few hours of sleep have at least restored some clarity to his mind.

"You mind watching a couple hours?" Horvath asks. "I could really use some z's."

"Sure, no sweat. Knock yourself out."

Horvath wraps himself in his poncho and liner and instantly falls asleep. As his snores rise from the bottom of the hole, Andy feels a wave of affection for the Hungarian refugee. God knows why, but Horvath is making it his business to keep him alive. Staring over the barrel of his rifle into the impenetrable gloom beyond the perimeter, Andy is tired, but he knows he will not sleep. He has the watch, and he will not, under any circumstances, let his buddy down.

He has survived his first combat without disgracing himself, and he now sees that from the moment he set foot in the recruiting office, he has been part of a process that has led him to this spot as surely as if he were on a conveyer belt. He has been fed, clothed, sheltered and allowed to enjoy the company of his fellows while they have been conditioned to unquestioning obedience, and have been herded like cattle to the slaughterhouse. Would he do it all over again, knowing what he knows now? That is hard to say and is, essentially, irrelevant. His task now is to survive.

An all-too-familiar gurgling starts in his lower abdomen. To make an already unpleasant situation even more uncomfortable, the daily malaria pills have given him the runs. Boot camp and AIT have conditioned him to a lack of privacy, but he still feels squeamish when it is necessary to take a shit with others watching. Now, at least, he has the cover of darkness. As the stabbing cramps begin, he grabs an entrenching tool and climbs out of the hole and gets behind a bush a few yards away. He barely has time to get his trousers down and squat, before the diarrhea explodes from him in a liquid rush.

Although the sky is overcast and rain is falling, there is a good deal of ambient light, for the moon is out behind the clouds. Cottony mist hangs low over the flooded paddies, and it occurs to him that a thousand NVA regulars could be creeping towards him in his vulnerable position. Someone coughs a few meters away. Looking toward the sound, he sees the glow of a cigarette cupped in a trooper's hand. Stupid, he thinks. He has half a mind to shoot the idiot himself. After cleaning himself up and burying his mess, he creeps back to his foxhole.

What time is it now, back in the World? It is still yesterday, he figures, sometime in the afternoon. He thinks of his family: his father, hard-working and patriotic, so proud to have a son who is "doing his part"; his mother, whose hugs he pretended to dislike, but really treasured; and his kid sister just going into fifth grade. He thinks about cars and round-eyed girls, clean sheets and flush toilets and hot water coming out of the tap. These ordinary things, so long taken for granted, are now beyond priceless. He imagines going to the refrigerator and drinking cold milk right from the carton while he eats a Devil Dog. This is the food that symbolizes for him everything that the World has to offer; not steak or hamburger or his mom's tollhouse cookies or apple pie. He would give his soul for a Devil Dog right now, to bite into the rich devil's food cake and feel the explosion of sweet, creamy filling at the back of his tongue. He resolves that in his next letter home, he will ask them to send him a box of the snack cakes.

Horvath has advised him to stop thinking about home, but that is easier said than done. How do you stop thinking about something, when the harder you try to forget it, the more you are reminded of it? In the long, dreary hours of the night, events of his life come back to him, incidents long forgotten and now recalled in vivid detail.

There was a gang of boys in his neighborhood who called themselves, not too imaginatively, the "Hellraisers." Their ringleader was a boy a few years older than he named Jimmy MacTavish. Red-haired and freckled, with a merry gap-toothed grin, Jimmy was both tough and charismatic, a charming rogue. Everyone said that he would either wind up a hero or in jail.

One sparkling morning in May, Jimmy MacTavish and two of his henchmen, Paul Sullivan and Russell Overmeier, came by Andy's house on their bicycles. He was on his lawn playing with a frisbee, when Jimmy called out to him.

"Hey, wuss! Ya wanna ride with us?"

To be invited to accompany the older boys was a great honor and a great thrill. It did not occur to Andy that Jimmy MacTavish might have some ulterior motive. He ran to get his bike.

They rode through the village and into the wooded hills on the outskirts of town, stopping at a chain link fence where a sign proclaimed in red letters:

DANGER
NO TRESPASSING

Andy knew what this place was, although he had never been inside the fence. It was famous. Two boys had actually died here in separate incidents. His parents had forbidden him to come to this place, and had made him swear that he would not. Now he was here, and already steeling himself for what he suspected was to come, for to shame himself in front of the Hellraisers would be far worse than breaking his vow.

They climbed the fence and followed a faint trail through the pine forest for a quarter mile, before stopping at the edge of a chasm. The railroad gorge had been blasted through the granite of the hill. It was probably no more than seventy-five feet deep, but to Andy, looking down, it seemed a thousand.

"We've had our eye on you, wuss," Jimmy told him. "We think you might be Hellraiser material. Right, guys?"

Russ and Sully smirked and nodded enthusiastically.

"But if you want to join our gang, you gotta pass the initiation test. You gotta climb down to the train tracks and back up again."

"Are you guys gonna do it too?"

"We've already done it, wuss."

Somehow he doubted that, but there was nothing to be gained by challenging Jimmy's truthfulness. He had a simple choice: accept the challenge, or chicken out.

"Okay," he said.

The boys became strangely quiet when they realized he was actually going to do it. They seemed to be holding their collective breath as he lowered himself over the edge and started down the cliff. The blasting had left the rock jagged, and there were numerous crevices and protrusions where he could get a grip. He tried not to think of the chasm yawning below him, and to concentrate on where he was placing his hands and feet. There was a bad moment when he slipped on some loose rock. He dislodged a chunk of granite, and as he watched it fall down, down into the abyss, he imagined his own body following the same path. The horror of it caused him to freeze and cling to the rock face for dear life.

"What's taking you so long, wuss?" Jimmy taunted him.

The sneer in Jimmy's voice provided the necessary impetus to get him going again. Sweat made his palms slick and ran stinging into his eyes, as he scratched and clawed his way to the bottom of the cliff and stood on the railroad tracks looking up at the boys far above him.

"Whattaya waitin' for?" Jimmy called. "Get back up here."

Climbing back up the cliff actually was easier than descending, because he did not have to look down. He made steady progress, and at last hauled himself over the lip of the gorge and lay on the ground, too physically and emotionally spent to move. But he had done it- he was now a Hellraiser!

Jimmy extended a hand to help him to his feet.

"Not bad, wuss, a little slow, but not bad at all. I gotta admit I'm surprised. Did I say that was the test? No, this is the test: Do it again."

It was too much. It was not fair. As he ran away, back to the spot where he had left his bike, the boys' laughter and shouts of "Chicken!" rang shamefully in his ears. He had done it, he told himself, he had nothing more to prove. But no matter how many times he told himself this, a niggling voice deep down inside told him it was not so. The truth was, Jimmy MacTavish had his number.

As it turned out, Jimmy fulfilled both of the destinies that had been predicted for him. He did time in reform school for burglarizing a Texaco station, and he was also the first in their town to come home from the Nam in a shiny aluminum coffin. Andy has survived his first time in combat, and although he had not distinguished himself, he had not disgraced himself either. But here there is no walking away. This test will go on for 365 days, if he is lucky enough to survive that long. As he remembers him now, it seems that Jimmy MacTavish is laughing at him.

*

In the morning, Alpha Company enters the village, which consists of perhaps a dozen thatched-roof huts arranged in a semi-circle about a central square. There are pens holding livestock, and ducks and chickens and skinny yellow dogs wander about freely. Of the human occupants there is no sign, but Andy has a distinct sensation of many pairs of eyes following him as he walks past the houses, locked and cocked, alert for any hint of trouble.

Some wise guy has decorated the front of his helmet with a pattern of concentric rings forming a target, with the bullet hole from yesterday's firefight piercing the bullseye. Although he made a show of squawking about it when he discovered it, secretly Andy is pleased. He feels that the target gives him a certain cachet. It makes him feel "bad."

One side of the village square is occupied by a one-storey cement structure with an empty flagpole that dates back to French colonial days. The company CP has been set up under the eaves of this building. Captain Roth is there, a sad-eyed bear of a man in rumpled jungle fatigues with a heavy growth of beard darkening his jaw. First Sergeant Sanchez is with him, looking as neat as the captain is slovenly, and also Jean Francoeur, his RTO, Doc Petersen, the company medic, and a tall, rangy lieutenant Andy has not seen before. When he asks who the officer is, he is told it is the artillery forward observer who called in the supporting fire that saved their bacon on the previous day.

Third Platoon is given the job of searching the village, while the other platoons provide security. The men have done this many times before, and they fan out in practiced fashion, ignoring the yelling and hand-waving of Lt. Berry, who is trying ineffectually to direct the proceedings. The shouts of the troopers succeed in bringing forth the villagers from their homes. They come out hesitantly, old men, women and children, no males of military age. They are herded around the flagpole in the courtyard, where they squat on their haunches under the watchful gaze of a pair of troopers.

There is little evidence of yesterday's artillery bombardment, which is surprising, as many of the shells fell directly in the village. Confirmation of this is provided by an old woman who is found lying in one of the houses with her legs terribly shredded by shrapnel. Doc Petersen treats her wounds, and it is decided to call a medevac chopper to take her to a hospital.

Andy follows Horvath into one of the Vietnamese hooches. His first impression is how pleasantly snug and dry it is inside. As his eyes adjust to the dim interior, he sees that he is in a large room, sparsely furnished, with a Buddhist shrine occupying a prominent position at the far end. He stands there, unsure of what to do with himself, as Horvath climbs up onto a table to poke around under the eaves.

"Nothing here," Horvath says.

A sound reaches Andy's ears, faint but distinct, like the scuttling of a small animal.

"I heard something," he says.

Horvath jumps down, his eyes darting to the corners of the room.

"You sure?"

"Pretty sure, but I don't know where it came from. It sounded almost like it was beneath my feet."

"Sometimes these places have cellars."

Horvath pulls back the rice straw mat that covers a portion of the dirt floor, and a trap door is exposed. He lifts off the wooden cover, and laying it to one side, points his rifle into the dark hole.

"*Lai dai!*" He calls. "Come out!"

There is only silence from the hole. Lt. Berry appears in the doorway of the house. He has followed them in, and sees immediately what is going on.

"Frag it," he orders.

Horvath turns his head toward the lieutenant, a surprised expression on his face.

"No way, sir. I think there's people down there."

"Okay, check it out if you want to. It's your funeral. But hurry it up, we've got a schedule to meet."

Horvath takes off his helmet and pack and lowers himself cautiously into the hole. The muffled sound of his voice can be heard, speaking in soothing tones. Then his head and shoulders re-emerge through the trap door.

"They're coming out," he says.

Horvath hauls himself out of the hole, followed by three teen-age girls in black pajamas. Their faces are flat, their hair lank and stringy. None of them is particularly attractive, but they are nubile, and it is easy to understand why they were hidden from the GI's.

"All right," says Lt. Berry, "get them over with the others."

When Andy takes the arm of one of the girls, offering what he intends as a sympathetic smile, she flinches violently away from his touch and gives him a look of pure, naked hatred. He has never been looked at in that way before, and his first reaction is to feel hurt. His hurt, however, quickly turns to anger.

82

Ungrateful bitch, he thinks, *doesn't she realize that we just saved her life?*

The girls are greeted with wolf whistles when Andy and Horvath escort them across the courtyard. They squat on their heels amid the other villagers, with the rain soaking through their black pajamas and plastering their hair to their scalps.

Horvath asks one of the guards if the cement building has been checked out yet. The man says he thinks so, but is not sure.

"Come on," Horvath says to Andy, "this might be interesting. Let's take a look inside."

They pass through the door of the building and enter what is apparently a classroom. Chairs equipped with writing arms are arranged in neat rows before a teacher's desk, facing a blackboard that takes up much of the wall. The blackboard is covered with children's drawings. At the top, a technically correct rendition of a B-52 defecates a stream of bombs upon a village whose inhabitants are shown cowering, fleeing, being blown to pieces, their faces contorted with terror and agony. In the foreground, a mother kneels beside her dead child, and an old man in a conical hat gazes up at the aircraft with his palms spread in a gesture of futility. Off to one side, a macabre caricature of an American soldier, a monster with bulging eyes and dripping fangs, smiles upon the devastation.

"I don't think these people like us very much," Andy observes.

"You got that right," Horvath says. "Take a look at this."

He has opened the teacher's desk drawer and removed a square of red cloth, which he lifts up and lets unfold to its full size. It proves to be a red flag displaying the yellow Soviet hammer and sickle.

"This is Charlie Cong country," says Horvath, "and there ain't no doubt about it."

Horvath tucks the flag away in his pack as a souvenir. Andy picks up an eraser resting on a shelf below the blackboard. He is about to wipe away the drawing, but Horvath stops him.

"Leave it," he says. "It might be good for some of our guys to see what they think of us."

At the sound of shouting, the two troopers hurry back outside. Someone has discovered a cache of rice, huge clay jars filled with the grain, stored in a barn near the livestock pens. As one of their purposes is the interdiction of Charlie's food supply, Captain Roth orders that the rice be destroyed. With the rain falling now in sheets, this proves to be no easy task. It is finally decided to pour the rice into a heap and to set fire to the barn, after filling it up with straw and pieces of furniture.

A roaring inferno ensues, and as the flames leap high and smoke billows skyward, a great wailing rises from the villagers. Their food is being destroyed, and sparks are flying from the barn and landing on neighboring roofs. Soon several houses are also ablaze. Some of the villagers try to rescue their property, but they are held back by the armed troopers.

"We oughtta waste ever' last one of these zipperheads," opines the Preacher.

The looks on the men's faces indicate that there are few who would disagree with him. Sergeant Roundtree was a popular NCO.

Finally Captain Roth is satisfied that the rice has been destroyed, and gives the order to abandon the village. As they trudge away through the rain, leaving ruin and suffering behind them, Andy turns and looks back toward the burning village.

"Goddamnit," he cries, "those are people's houses back there!"

"Take it easy, man," Snake advises. "This is what you signed up for. Join the Army and see the world. Travel to exotic places. Meet new and interesting people. And kill them."

*

There will be no rest for the weary. When they finally stop for the day, Dingle Berry decides that he does not like the look of some buildings that can be seen above them on a hillside. He sends the Third Squad up to check them out.

They find a compound of simple dwellings clustered around a quaint structure with three tiers of upswept roofs rising to a pointed peak. As they walk into the place, Andy gets a strange feeling, as if he has stepped out of space and time into a different dimension. Under the circumstances, it is not a pleasant feeling, almost like discovering that someone has spiked your drinking water with a hallucinogenic drug.

When the residents of the place come out to meet them, they remind Andy of pictures drawn by people who claim to have seen visitors from outer space. At first glance, they seem as alike as peas in a pod, with shaven heads and identical saffron robes. Upon closer inspection, though, they prove to be of all shapes and sizes, and to range in age from young to truly ancient.

Correctly identifying Bird Lawler as the leader of the Americans, the eldest of the group approaches him and bows formally with his hands steepled together. This one is smiling politely, but the faces of the others, huddled together in a tight bunch, are impassive and give away nothing.

"What'll we do with 'em, Bird?" Snake asks. "Should we round 'em up?"

"I dunno," Bird says uncertainly. "These guys look like some kind of religious group."

"That's right," Horvath confirms. "They're Buddhist monks, noncombatants. This here is a temple."

"Ain't no such thing as a 'noncombatant.' For my money, they're all a bunch a VC."

The Preacher's eyes are darting from one monk to another, as he looks for the slightest excuse to blow the entire group away.

"Tell you what," says Bird, "let's take a look in their hooches and see what we come up with. Then we'll decide what to do with 'em."

Searching the living quarters, they find rice mats for sleeping, jugs of water and some extra robes. There is a kitchen with a stove and some cooking pots, a mess hall with rice bowls laid out in rows on the floor. The search turns up nothing of military significance.

"That don't prove nothing," Preacher insists. "All it proves is that they got their black pajamas and their AK's hid somewheres we ain't never gonna find 'em."

They enter the pagoda. Its interior is cool and dark, with massive teak beams supporting the elaborate structure of the roof. The air is sweet with the scent of incense. Red and yellow wall hangings display what appear to be large Chinese characters. On a dais facing the entrance rests a small bronze statue depicting a slim young man dressed in robes and wearing an ornate headdress like a crown. He sits with his knees apart and with his ankles crossed and tucked in his lap. His left palm lies open, and above it the right hand is held up with the fingers pointing to his chin. With his eyes closed and his lips pressed together in a mysterious smile, he gives off an aura of peace.

"Graven image!" spits Preacher, his eyes burning with outrage.

Hot Rod's eyes are alight with something more like avarice.

"That thing must be worth a fuckin' fortune!"

He walks up to the statue and hefts it, lifting it from the dais.

"Heavy," he grunts. "Must weigh a hundred pounds. But I bet I can hump it in my pack for a few days. It won't be long before we go back to base camp."

"Put it down!"

Andy did not intend to speak, and is amazed to hear his own voice echoing in the chamber. Hot Rod turns on him angrily.

"What say, cherry?"

"I said put the statue down. You can't take it. It's wrong."

"Wrong? I'll tell you what's wrong! What's wrong is me bustin' my hump for these zipperheads and puttin' my ass on the line for twelve fuckin' months. An' what do I get for it? Zip, that's what! You gonna make me put it down, cherry? You an' who else?"

"Me, Hot Rod," Horvath says quietly. "The cherry is right. What you got there is a Buddha statue. It would be like stealing a statue of Christ out of a church."

"This ain't no Buddha," Hot Rod grumbles. "Buddha is fat."

"I'm telling you," Horvath insists, "that is a Buddha."

"You can't hump that thing," Snake puts in reasonably. "You'll just wear yourself out carryin' it and wind up leavin' it beside the trail somewheres."

"It's the Devil's work," adds the Preacher. "It's a sin to touch it."

Hot Rod reluctantly bows to the will of the majority.

"All right," he says, "I'll leave the damn thing. But I'm tellin' you guys, I'm gonna regret this the rest a my fuckin' life."

*

When Bird gets the lieutenant on the horn and reports the situation, he is instructed to leave the monks in peace. The men of Third Squad descend the mountain slope and return to their company's encampment. As a reward for going on the patrol, Dingle Berry exempts them from perimeter guard duty. They will all get a good night's sleep tonight.

After they have dug their holes and cleaned their weapons and eaten their C's, there is a rare opportunity for them to relax together as a group. They lie under their jury-rigged shelters, smoking cigarettes and shooting the breeze. It is a pleasant and congenial time, and it reminds Andy of the late night bull sessions he used to share with his roommates in college.

"I bet you," Hot Rod is saying, "that right now all a them monkeys 're out snoopin' and poopin' an' doin' all kinds a bad shit."

"You got that wrong, man," says Horvath. "They're 'monks,' not 'monkeys,' and they're for real. They're antiwar, that's true. They're the guys that were setting themselves on fire in the streets of Saigon when the war was starting to heat up. But they're noncombatants, not for any side."

"Bullshit!" says Hot Rod. "You're tellin' me that a bunch a guys of military age can just sit out the war up there doin' nothing but prayin'. Bullshit! How do they get out of the draft, answer me that?"

"There's somethin' funny about a bunch a guys wearin' dresses and livin' together without no women," Snake puts in. If you ask me, they're all a bunch a queers."

This provokes a general snicker, as each of the men forms his own mental picture of the monks engaging in creative acts of buggery.

"Godless heathen!" Preacher exclaims. "Sodomites! Worshipers of graven images!"

"Hey," Andy pipes up, "Maybe the god they worship is the right one. Who knows, maybe there isn't any God at all."

Four pairs of eyes stare at him in utter shock. The Preacher is the first to break the silence.

"Satan," he hisses. "I knowed all along there was something about you. I thought you was from God, but now I know you. 'Get thee behind me, Satan!'"

"Hey," Andy protests, "take it easy. "No big deal, all right?"

But he finds no support from the others in this instance, not even from Horvath. Their eyes are hard as they look at him, and he tells himself that he must remember never to let his guard down, that this is not college, and the next time he thinks about speaking his mind to keep his damn mouth shut.

*

The next day Alpha Company remains in place. The cloud cover is too low for them to be moved by air, and it is decided that their present position can be used as a base for running ambush patrols. Dingle Berry passes this happy news along to the men, and advises them to get some rest, as they are likely to be in for a long evening.

They keep themselves as dry as they can under their makeshift shelters, amusing themselves by watching the parade of villagers whose homes they burned the day before, and who have now been turned into refugees. All day long, these people straggle past the perimeter in small groups, driving their livestock and carrying whatever belongings they have managed to salvage in carts or on their backs.

In the middle of the afternoon they are treated to an extraordinary sight. An old man wearing black pajamas and a conical hat is walking along with a monkey perched on his shoulder. Several paces behind him a woman, presumably his wife, is bent beneath a gigantic load of household goods to which are tied a flock of chickens. The blanket of birds flapping and fluttering on her back makes the old woman look like a giant chicken herself. The men are laughing and pointing, joking about the spectacle of the henpecked wife, when Snake Holloway waves his arms to attract the old man's attention and calls to him:

"Hey, old timer, *lai dai*! Come here!"

The old man obligingly approaches, smiling eagerly, followed by the heavily laden woman. When they reach the perimeter, Jason Ash climbs out of his foxhole and covers them with his rifle. Always wary of anyone who is not wearing an American uniform, the Preacher is taking no chances.

Snake walks over to the old woman, who is standing quietly under her load like a beast of burden, and points to one of the chickens. Taking a pack of cigarettes from his pocket, he gestures first to the chicken and then to the cigarettes.

"Smokes for chicken," he says, "hokay?"

The old man's face splits in a betel-stained grin, and he lets loose a stream of unintelligible Vietnamese. In the meantime the monkey, which has hopped from his shoulder down to the ground, runs over to the Preacher and hugs him about the leg.

"Stupid old geezer," Snake snarls, "you don't understand a word I'm saying, do you? Hey, Preacher," he adds, "looks like you got yourself a friend there."

Jason Ash looks down at the monkey, which is now vigorously rubbing itself against his shin. It takes him a moment to realize that the critter is humping him.

"GIT OFFA ME!" he roars. "QUIT THAT, YOU DURN LITTLE HOMO!"

The old man is hopping from one foot to the other, cackling with mirth. Having the dink laughing at him enrages the Preacher even more. Kicking the monkey violently away from him, he levels his rifle and fires. The M-14 round catches the monkey squarely in the chest and flings it back several feet, where it lies twitching on the ground. The movement is purely reflexive; its head and shoulders have been blown almost completely away. The old man is no longer laughing. He bends down and gently touches the lifeless form of his pet.

"Git outta here," Snake tells him.

With his sheath knife, he cuts the thong binding the chicken to the woman's back.

"Go on, vamoose, *didi mau*!"

The old couple shuffle hurriedly away, the man trembling with fear, the woman struggling to keep up with him under her heavy load. As Jason Ash retrieves the monkey's carcass, presumably planning to cook and eat it, Snake shakes his head sadly.

"Pore litto feller," he intones with mock solemnity. "He died fer love."

*

The men of Third Squad are preparing for the ambush patrol for which Dingle Berry has "volunteered" them.

"Helmets, but no packs," he told them. "Each rifleman will carry ten magazines, four frags, a trip flare and a claymore mine. You can pick up the claymores and the flares at the company CP. No aftershave or bug juice- you know the drill. Be ready to move out at 1800 hours."

They curse the lieutenant for this latest misery to be inflicted on them, but the complaining is just letting off steam. They know that Dingle Berry is not responsible; that the order had come from the captain. They clean their weapons, then pad and tape their equipment so there will be no sounds of metal striking metal. They put bits of foliage in the slits in the camouflage covers to break up the round silhouettes of their helmets. They do not apply face paint, which they consider to be "Mickey Mouse." After going to the CP to draw the claymores, anti-personnel mines which use a C-4 charge to hurl balls of steel forward over a sixty-degree arc, they settle down to grab whatever rest they can.

Andy has taped his dogtags together so they will not jingle. He has taped the sheath of his bayonet and the sling swivels of his rifle. The ammo pouches that he carries were designed for the larger M-14 magazines, so he has stuffed in crumpled cardboard from C-ration boxes to keep the magazines from rattling.

He has paid particular attention to the grenades that are secured by straps to his ammo pouches, taping the pull rings and the spoons so there is no possibility of anything moving. When Horvath comes to check him over, he laughs at what he has done with the grenades.

"You're gonna have a heck of a time getting those loose if you need 'em."

Andy has never liked grenades. He has been afraid of them ever since he was first exposed to them in basic training.

"I don't want to have an accident like that Lieutenant Cushman, or whatever his name was."

"Andy, I gotta tell you something. When we say that somebody 'had an accident with a hand grenade,' that don't usually mean there was an accident. It's like a euphonism, you get my meaning?"

Andy does get Horvath's meaning, and it makes him feel queasy.

"Now let me show you what to do with those grenades," Horvath continues. "You can put a little tape on the ring so it won't rattle, but make sure you leave it free so you can pull it. Now, straighten out half of the pin to make it easier to pull, but leave the other half bent so it won't come out by accident, okay?"

"Okay, boss, I got it."

*

They set out in the early evening, traveling light and moving fast, two rifle squads from the Third Platoon reinforced by a pair of machine gun crews from the Weapons Platoon, all under Dingle Berry's command. After moving along the edge of the paddies for a few klicks, they climb into the foothills to a plateau blanketed by elephant grass. The rain is cold and stinging, driven by a wind that keeps the tall stalks moving in constant, sinuous motion.

The elephant grass eventually gives way to a forest of small and medium-sized trees. Here the pace is slowed, and the patrol moves with great caution, stopping frequently to look and listen. During one of these pauses, Andy hears the sound of water. They creep forward to the edge of a gully and look down at a rushing stream. Several yards downstream, there is a bamboo bridge and a path leading to a small hamlet.

At Lt. Berry's signal, the troopers descend the embankment to place their flares and claymores along the trail, then scramble back up, trailing the detonator wires behind them. They find positions of concealment outside the area of the mines' backblast, and settle down in the gathering twilight for what promises to be a long wait.

Andy is positioned near the end of the line farthest from the bridge, between Snake Holloway and a machine gun that has been put out to provide flank security. Unbeknownst to the rest of his team, he has screwed up badly, tripping over a fallen log and jamming the barrel of his rifle into the mud. The muzzle is clogged, and as they are now in silence mode, he cannot take the steps necessary to clear it. If he has to face Charlie, it will be with his bare hands.

Time slows to an agonizing crawl, each moment like a drop of molasses dangling on a gossamer thread before falling away into oblivion. Andy is soaked to the skin. Cold creeps into his bones, and hunger gnaws at his belly. He cannot decide which is worse, his craving for a cigarette, or his need to urinate. The luminous hands of his watch are both standing up straight, when he decides that Charlie is not coming.

After midnight the rain stops, and in its place come hordes of hungry mosquitoes. The men have not been allowed to use insect repellent, because the smell might give them away. Andy makes a kind of game out of seeing how long he can endure their bites before reaching to pinch them between thumb and forefinger.

What time is it now, back in the World? Late morning, he guesses, or early afternoon. He wonders what Joan Munson is doing right now, and decides that she is probably lying in the sun beside the swimming pool at the Valley View Country Club. Picturing her in her two-piece bathing suit, her tawny blond hair fanned out over the golden-brown skin of her back, he is filled with a longing so piercing that he almost cries out from the agony of it.

He snaps back to reality with a throbbing erection, annoyed with himself for allowing his mind to wander. There are no sounds but the peeep-peeep of tree frogs, repetitive fuck-you's from a nearby gekko, the whine of mosquitoes, the burble of the stream. Occasionally there is a faint pshhhhht of the radio breaking squelch to signal that they are still on station. A few yards to his left, Snake's silhouette is so still, he wonders if he might be asleep.

A different sound reaches his ears, one that does not fit with the natural pattern. Was he mistaken? No, there it is again, a faint singsong barely audible above the gurgle of the stream. Snake has heard it too. His head cocks sideways, and the rifle in his hands lifts perceptibly.

A group of people is approaching the bridge from the south. Secure in the belief that the countryside belongs to them at night, they are jabbering like girl scouts at a picnic. It sounds as if there are a lot of them, and remembering his useless weapon, Andy has an almost uncontrollable urge to jump up and run.

He sees them now, dark shadows moving in a pack along the trail. The group pauses, and one of the shadows detaches itself and approaches the spot where Andy and Snake are hiding. He is only a few feet away from them, and it seems impossible that he cannot see them. Andy holds his breath. His heart is hammering, and he is trembling so violently, he fears that the rattle of his equipment will give him away. The VC leans his rifle against a tree and fumbles with his trousers. As piss splashes copiously on the ground, Andy's own overstressed bladder lets go.

While continuing to urinate, the VC turns his head and calls something back over his shoulder. That is when Snake shoots him, firing a burst that lifts him off the ground and throws him over backward. A hail of fire erupts from the ambush positions, as streams of red tracers follow the enemy running back along the trail.

"CEASE FIRE! CEASE FIRE!"

At the screams from the lieutenant, the firing dwindles, and all is quiet again. Andy hears the sound of someone crashing through the brush. Dingle Berry is approaching, and he is furious.

"What the fuck happened here?" he screams. "The orders were that I would trigger the ambush- nobody but me!"

Snake rises up from his hiding place to answer the lieutenant.

"It was the new man, sir. One of the dinks came over here to take a piss, and the cherry just up and shot him. Can't say as I blame him, sir."

Andy cannot believe his ears. Snake, his buddy, is putting the blame on him. He is frozen, too stunned to speak.

"Goddamnit, Cullen," the lieutenant explodes, "you could fuck up a wet dream! You'll be lucky if I don't court martial you! Now everyone within five miles knows our location. For all we know, that bunch might have been the lead element for a PAVN regiment. Lissen up, everybody - blow the claymores. We're getting the fuck outta here!"

*

"Andy," Horvath says, "I gotta talk to you."

After returning from the aborted ambush, the two have spent the rest of the night under a shelter hastily constructed next to their hole, the bottom of which is full of water. It is another morning in the Nam, and they are using one of their last heat tabs to boil water for coffee.

"Look," Horvath says, "I can understand why you wasted that dink, he was practically peeing on you for Chrissake. But the guys didn't like it. They think you might 've got some of us killed out there. What I'm saying is, we got a problem. Some of the guys are saying you oughtta be DX'd."

Andy knows that the acronym "DX" stands for "direct exchange." It is applied to the process of turning in an item of clothing or equipment for a similar item, as in, "Go down to supply and DX that old field jacket." He has never heard the term applied to an individual, and it takes him a moment to catch Horvath's drift.

"Now, wait just a goddamn minute!"

"I've been trying to get them to back off," Horvath continues. "Snake wants to cut you some slack, but Hot Rod and the Preacher have a hard-on for you."

"How about Bird?"

"Bird ain't in on it, on account of him being the squad leader. He's probably got an idea what's going on, but nobody's talking to him about it."

"Anton, I didn't shoot that VC. Snake did."

"Hey look, Andy, I already told you, it's okay. I understand."

"No, really. I didn't shoot him. I didn't shoot anybody. I didn't even fire my rifle at all last night."

"Are you shitting me? 'Cause if you are...."

"When we were climbing back up after we put out the claymores, I tripped and got the barrel of my rifle clogged with dirt. I couldn't fire it."

"Why didn't you say anything, for Chrissake?"

"I was surprised when Snake said it was me who did the shooting. And, well, I guess I didn't want to look stupid."

"You'd die before you let yourself look stupid?"

"Hey, I didn't have any idea that it could come to that."

"Have you cleaned your rifle yet?"

"No, I was too tired. I know I should have, but I decided I could do it this morning."

"Let me have a look at it."

Andy hands over his M-16. After ejecting the magazine and working the loading handle to confirm that the chamber is clear,

93

Horvath tips the weapon up to inspect the muzzle. Then, pulling the handle back again, he bends down and sniffs the open breech.

"Jesus Christ," he says. "Let me see your ammo pouches."

Andy picks up his web gear and gives it to Horvath.

"It's all there," he says. "I didn't fire a single round."

A quick inspection is all that is required to confirm that he is telling the truth.

"We are gonna get this goddamn business straightened out," Horvath says, "right goddamn now! Snake," he shouts, "where the hell are you?"

Snake detaches himself from a group of troopers and walks over to them.

"Whatchew want, Horvath?"

"Snake, what do you mean, telling everyone that it was Andy who shot that Cong last night? I just checked his weapon. It's plugged with mud. It was never even fired."

"Aw, he could a plugged it any time."

"I'm telling you it wasn't fired! I checked it, and I also checked to see if he's still got all of his ammo, and he does!"

Horvath is shouting, and the noise attracts the attention of everyone in the vicinity. Heads are turning, and guys are moving closer to see what is going on.

"That's pretty low, Snake, blaming a cherry for something you did. You could a got him killed, for Chrissake."

The jig is up, and Snake knows it. He backpedals, trying to make the best of a bad situation.

"I wouldn't a let nuthin' happen to him. I was trying to talk the boys into lettin' him off easy. I'd a told 'em if they kep' on talkin' 'bout DXin' him."

"Well, you tell them now, Snake, or I will. Jesus, man, you have become fuckin' worthless since you got short. We'd be better off if you just got the hell out of here."

"Aw, God I know it!" Snake moans. "I ain't no good to nobody. I tried to tell the sarge that, but he wouldn't listen. He made me come out here anyway."

He is blubbering now, the tears making tracks down his dirty cheeks. The troopers who have been attracted by the spectacle turn away from him in embarrassment and disgust.

VII. ONE GOOD THING

Thirteen days. Thirteen days of slogging through paddies, of searching villages where stony-eyed Viets looked at them as if they were from Mars. Thirteen days of never being dry, of water, water everywhere, but not a drop of it drinkable, of feet painfully chafed by their boots and cracked from immersion, of eating cold C-rations and sleeping in the mud. And all this time, never knowing when the bullets will start to fly or a booby trap explode, never knowing if the next moment might be their last.

After the first two days of Operation Paul Revere II, A Company has had no further contact with the enemy, although they have found lots of rice and burned lots of thatch. Rumor has it that other Cav elements are in heavy contact in the jungle near the Cambodian border, but in their sector on the coastal plain, Charlie has vanished. When word comes down that they are returning to base camp to rest and refit, the news is received with jubilation.

On the morning of the fourteenth day, the slicks come for them. Andy hops aboard with practiced ease. Over the course of the past two weeks they have been airlifted several times, hopscotching around looking for Charlie, and the procedure has become second nature to him.

In less than an hour the familiar shape of Hon Cong Mountain, with the Cav's emblem painted on its crest, appears below, and they come swooping down onto the Golf Course. Trucks are there to meet them and transport them back to their company area. There is a brief company formation, in which Captain Roth tells them they have done a fine job and he is proud of them. They are to turn in their ammo at supply, and then go to the mess hall, where there is hot chow waiting for them. After chow there will be a movie, *Charlie Brown's Christmas*. As a reward for their performance, they are to have the next twenty-four hours off. The men's whoop when they are dismissed is reminiscent of their innocent days in basic training.

At the mess hall the cooks are waiting with mermite cans of stew, freshly baked bread and lemonade, and ice cream for dessert. The "ice cream" consists of powdered milk and food coloring. It is rumored to be the brainchild of a lieutenant in graves registration and to have been made utilizing the refrigeration facilities of the morgue. It leaves a chalky aftertaste, but it is cold and unbelievably delicious. Andy eats a gallon of the stuff before staggering back to the Third Platoon's hooch, where he strips off his filthy fatigues and leaves them on the floor. He falls onto his cot, tucks the mosquito netting beneath him, and is out like a light.

*

When Andy awakes, the hooch is deserted. A glance at his watch tells him that it is midmorning. He has slept almost fifteen hours. Base camp is an oasis in the midst of chaos. Although Charlie might lob in a random mortar round now and then, there is no chance that he will launch an attack against its formidable defenses. In the war's deadly game it is a safety zone, where a man is not likely either to be tagged or bagged. It is wonderful to feel safe. He rolls out of the rack and stumbles groggily outside to the piss tube, where he takes a long and satisfying whizz. Returning to the barracks, he rummages in his locker for a bar of soap and a towel. He dons a pair of flipflops and walks along the duckboards to the shower building.

There is a full-length mirror on the wall, of such poor quality it could have been used in a funhouse. But it is not the distortion that causes him to pause in shock at the sight of his own reflection. He has not seen himself in some time, and was not prepared for the changes that have occurred. His body looks like the pictures he has seen of World War Two concentration camp victims- he must have lost almost thirty pounds! His face is gaunt, the nose and cheekbones prominent, the eyes sunken, wild and watchful. The person in the mirror is a stranger, and in a strange way, he makes Andy feel afraid.

The water in the shower is lukewarm, the immersion heater on the roof of the building having been on for only a short while, but it is warm enough to be comfortable. He steps under the stream and rubs the soap over his neck and arms. It is unbelievable how dirty he is. As he scrubs, the water running off him turns brown, and the true color of his skin shows through in mottled patches. He is working up a lather in his hair, enjoying the sensation of the water coursing down his back, when someone shouts outside:

"Who is using this shower?"

He pushes the door open, and is confronted by Rocco DiFazio, the battalion supply sergeant, risen to his full height of five feet, four inches, and obviously angry.

"Young man, turn off that water!"

Andy hastens to comply.

"Now, since being considerate would obviously not occur to you, I am going to instruct you as to how we do things around here. We only run the hot water in the shower when we have to. We get wet. We turn it off. We lather up. We rinse. Then we turn it off, and we are done. That way, everybody gets his fair share of the hot water. Is that clear, young man?"

"Yes, sergeant."

"Then get the hell out of my shower!"

Sergeant DiFazio turns on his heel and stalks off, leaving him standing there with soap in his eyes. Andy is furious. Fair share. That lifer dares to talk to him of "fair share?" Who has been using his fair share of the water for the last two weeks while he has been out risking his ass in the boonies? If Andy had known about the rule, he would have obeyed it. There was no reason to make him out to be an inconsiderate prick. He considers defying the sergeant and staying under the warm water awhile longer, but his enjoyment of the shower has been spoiled. He rinses the soap out of his hair and returns to the barracks.

As he is putting on a set of clean stateside fatigues, Horvath comes in carrying a stack of letters.

"Mail call," he says. "These are for you."

He scans the return addresses on the envelopes. Most are from his family, but there is a small pink one from Joan Munson.

"Hey, Andy," says Horvath, "a bunch of us are going down to the ville. The first sergeant has even sprung me. The jeep will be here in ten minutes. You want to come along?"

"Is Snake coming?"

"No, I ain't seen Snake this morning. I don't know where he is. Guess he's laying low."

"All right, then, I'm in. I'm gonna get some enjoyment out of this day, if it kills me."

*

Horvath has left him alone, and Andy prepares to open his mail from home. With only a few minutes before he will be going downtown, he has chosen three letters, one from his father as an appetizer, one from his little sister as the main course, and the one from Joan Munson for dessert. His father's letter is a rant against communism and the anti-war movement. After some choice words for the "Chinks" and the "Russkies" and the "long haired hippie faggots," he concludes with an anecdote about a man on his factory shift.

A few days ago Chet Nowacki's son ran off to Canada to avoid the draft. The poor guy is so ashamed he hasn't been coming to work because he doesn't want to face the guys. I don't know how I could take it if my son did something like that. I'm proud that my boy is a real American!

His father spent a couple of years in the Pacific as a Seabee. Although John Wayne made a movie called *The Fighting Seabees*, Andy doubts that his father's unit saw any serious combat. He suspects, in fact, that the old man does not have a clue as to what combat is about. He tosses the letter aside and picks up the one from his sister, Lucy. Her letter is chatty and filled with news of home, recounted with her usual irreverent humor.

I hope you don't mind, I've taken over your room. My old one was so much smaller. Don't worry, though, I'm keeping it just the same. (Except I threw out all your basketball trophies and painted the walls black.) Speaking of black, Raven really misses you. He's really sad, and whenever a car comes up the driveway he jumps up and runs to the door. I let him sleep with me, and that seems to make him feel better. I wish he wouldn't fart so darn much though....

Andy smiles and wipes away a tear. That kid, he thinks, is really something. In a few years the guys are going to be eating their hearts out. Speaking of which... he tears open the flimsy pink envelope.

Dear Andy,

It's hard to imagine this letter reaching you all the way on the other side of the world. I see awful things happening in Vietnam on the t.v. every night, and I hope you are not in the middle of them. There is a lot of talk here against the war. You're the only one I know who has gone. All the other boys I know either have student deferments or have figured out other ways to beat the draft. I haven't made up my mind yet whether I think it's right or wrong. It is all so confusing and I am very troubled by it. What do you think? That may be a stupid question to ask you, but it seems to me that you are more qualified than most to give an opinion because you are there and can see for yourself what is going on. I didn't realize how much I cared about you until I saw you in your uniform ready to go to that place. It was hard to believe it was you, so manly and serious and brave. It seems like just yesterday you were pulling my pigtails in Mrs. Hackett's geography class!

Please take care of yourself, Andy, and come home safe.

Your friend,
Joan

The net effect of the mail from home is to leave him feeling hurt and confused. The World is going on without him, and no one has the slightest understanding of what he is going through. Joan's letter, in particular, seems a betrayal. Like his father, she refers to increasingly widespread opposition to the war, and her own support appears ambiguous at best. She talks of "right or wrong" as if it is an abstract question in political science class. It does not matter whether he is here out of divine inspiration or human madness. He is here, in the Nam, and for him that is the only reality.

"Your friend" is hardly romantic, but she "cares for" him, and that at least is a start. He folds Joan's letter carefully and replaces it in the envelope.

*

Hot Rod is driving the jeep, and Bird is riding shotgun, with Andy and Horvath in the back seat. Hot Rod has received a bottle of tequila in a care package from home, and they are passing it around as they ride into the village of An Khe. Andy does not particularly like the taste of the cactus juice, but it goes down easily, and is more potent than it seemed at first. They are all hammered by the time they arrive downtown.

When they walk together through the gates of Sin City, they seem to have an aura about them. Rear echelon troops give them a wide berth on the wooden sidewalk. Andy can almost hear the theme song from *The Magnificent Seven* playing in the background.

Their first stop is the New York Bar, which is Bird and Horvath's favorite. It is true that the place is classier than the others on the strip, and the bar girls are pretty, but Andy's heart is set on renewing a previous acquaintance. After drinking a couple of beers with his squadmates, he excuses himself and goes in search of Lee. As he makes his way somewhat unsteadily towards the robin's-egg blue façade of the Houston Bar, he is distracted by a thumping Motown beat resonating from an open doorway.

The first thing he sees when he ducks inside is a skanky Viet go-go dancer in a miniskirt gyrating to James Brown's *Papa's Got a Brand New Bag*. The air is thick with marijuana smoke which is stirred, but not dispersed, by a slowly turning ceiling fan. He starts toward the bar, then pauses, realizing that all of the people in this place who are not Vietnamese are black. Horvath has warned him about the bars frequented exclusively by Negro soldiers, and he is about to beat a hasty retreat, when he catches sight of his friend Clarence Tyree seated at a table with a group of soul brothers.

Coming closer to the table, he thinks that he has been mistaken and that the man he has noticed is a Ty lookalike. But no, although his appearance has subtly changed, it is indeed his friend. Ty's face is haggard, the skin stretched taught over the bones. His military haircut has been allowed to grow out into something approaching an Afro. He wears a choker of wooden beads at his throat. His long fingers are delicately pinching a joint the size of a cigar.

"Hey, buddy," Andy cries, "how's it hanging?"

All heads in the room turn in his direction. Ty's eyes come blearily into focus on the pale-skinned intruder.

"Oh," he says, "it's you."

"Hey, bro'," asks a skinny fellow with a flattened nose and a mouthful of gold inlays, "yo' know dis rabbit?"

"Sure he knows me," Andy replies, placing a hand on Ty's shoulder. "We were in basic together."

Ty jerks violently away from his touch.

"Git away from me, Chuck!"

The look in his eyes is one that Andy has seen before. It is the same look that he has seen in the eyes of Viet villagers, a look of pure hatred. The murderous expressions on the others' faces are also chillingly familiar. Whether due to the quantity of alcohol that he has drunk, or some newly acquired toughness, Andy feels no fear. He has not completely lost his wits, though, and he knows that he must get out of this situation, and fast. He starts backing towards the door, keeping his eyes on Ty and the others at his table.

"Glad to see you're okay, man. You take care, now. I'll see you!"

Reaching the door, he turns tail and rushes outside. The brothers' laughter follows him, as he hurries along the sidewalk to the entrance to the Houston Bar. The place is more crowded than it was on his initial visit. All of the tables are occupied, and the air is filled with a buzz of conversation. He finds a seat at the bar, orders a 33 beer and asks the bartender if Lee is here. The old man shrugs in perfectly Gallic fashion.

"Many gel here, *monsieur, beaucoup* pretty gel. You stay Houston Bar and find numba one gel. *Cherchez la femme, n'est ce pas?*"

Andy picks up his beer and wanders among the tables, searching for Lee. A couple of girls approach him, but he waves them off. The noise, the crowd, the fetid smoky air make him feel dizzy and disoriented. The faces of the people at the tables appear wavering and distorted, as if he is seeing them underwater. Discouraged, he is ready to give up; and then he sees her.

She is wearing a white *ao dai*, the traditional Vietnamese dress with a tight, high-necked bodice and long slit skirt over silk pantaloons. Her glossy black hair is loose and falling to her waist. She is even more beautiful than he remembered, and his heart squeezes at the sight of her. She is sitting at a table in a far corner of the room with a skinny GI. Her companion looks like a typical Remington Raider, spectacled and chinless, with a shock of red hair and a ridiculous bushy moustache that fails to make him appear manly. The two are engaged in an intense conversation, laughing and chattering away like a pair of magpies. When she reaches out and touches the soldier's arm to emphasize a point, Andy's blood boils.

He walks over to the table, and Lee looks up at him with a confused smile that says she almost recognizes him, but not quite.

"Hello, Lee," he says.

"Hi, GI," she replies. "Lee busy now. You come back latah, ho-kay?"

"Not okay, honey. I only have a little time, and I really want to see you."

At this point the skinny soldier decides that it is time to assert his rights.

"Look, buddy, the lady is with me right now, okay?"

"Not okay, and I'm not your buddy, you fucking REMF!"

With a strength he had no idea he possessed, Andy grabs the soldier's collar with one hand and yanks him out of his chair. They are face to face, and the eyes behind the thick glasses are huge and wide with terror.

"All right," the soldier squeaks, "take it easy, man. I'm going."

Andy releases him, and he grabs his hat and scuttles away without a backward glance. Andy looks at Lee. There is fear in her eyes, and her small, sharp teeth are biting her lower lip; she is afraid of him. Well, he thinks, she is not the only one. He is actually afraid of himself.

"You go, GI," she says. "Get lost. *Didi mau.*"

"Look, Lee," he says, "I'm sorry. I've been in the boonies for the last couple of weeks, and I'll probably be going out again soon. I really wanted to see you. You remember me- Andy?"

As she continues to regard him warily, her expression softens.

"Ahn-dee. Yes, I 'membah. You damn quick, pshht-pshht. You want go boom-boom with Lee?"

"Yes, please."

"Hokay, Ahn-dee. You promise you be good boy, not hurt Lee, yes?"

"Baby, I wouldn't hurt you for anything in the world."

She rises from her chair, and leads the way through the curtain of bamboo beads and along the corridor to her room. He takes in the familiar surroundings: the bed, the washstand, the crucifix on the wall. *Jesus,* he thinks, *have you been enjoying the entertainment?*

Lee undresses and lies down on the bed with her knees raised. She seems more indifferent to him than last time he was with her. Under the circumstances, he supposes he can understand. He removes his own clothing and, finding himself ready, deals with the condom that he has remembered to bring with him. Joining her on the bed, he climbs on top of her without ceremony. He tries to kiss her, but she turns her face to the wall. She starts to move beneath him, rotating her hips and bucking with surprising energy.

Firmly in the saddle, Andy bangs away like a pile-driver. Although aroused, he feels numb, detached, and he finds that he is unable to achieve satisfaction. As their coupling goes on and on, Lee's mechanical motions subside and eventually cease altogether. She lies passive, indifferent, submitting to his incessant pounding. Andy, too, becomes tired of the exercise. At last, unable to continue the charade any longer, he stiffens, pretending to climax, and collapses on top of her.

She remains on the bed, watching him dully, as he dresses hurriedly and tosses a handful of MPC's on the washstand. Nude, she is exquisitely beautiful; yet her beauty does not move him. She cannot wait for him to go, and he cannot wait to leave. When he turns away to leave her little cubicle, she calls after him in an atrocious parody of a southern accent.

"Y'aw come back soon, y'heah?"

He rushes through the barroom, drawing curses as he bumps arms holding drinks, and bursts through the doorway. He barely makes it outside before falling to his knees and heaving the contents of his stomach over the sidewalk.

*

Returning to the New York Bar in search of his buddies, he does not find them there. He does, however, notice one familiar face. The red-haired soldier whom he separated forcibly from Lee is sitting at a table drinking a beer. And this time, he is not alone. He is accompanied by a half-dozen other fellows, some of whom, although plainly REMF's, are built like gorillas. They are positioned between him and the door, and as they push back their chairs and start towards him, there is time for only a single thought to penetrate the fog of his inebriated brain.

Oh, shit.

*

"Man, I gotta tell you, you look like shit warmed over."

Horvath is smiling down at him through the mosquito netting draped over his cot. Andy groans pitifully. He feels as if he has been run over by a truck. Every bone and muscle in his body hurts, and his head is splitting with a massive hangover. He tries to remember what

103

happened to him, but his mind is a blank.

"Those REMF's did quite a number on you," Horvath says. "The good news is there ain't no bones broken except your nose."

"What the hell happened?"

"I ain't sure exactly. When me and Bird came out of the back rooms at the New York Bar, a bunch a guys were putting the boots to you. You must of done something that really pissed them off. Anyway, we broke it up and got you outta there before the MP's came. We put you in the back of the jeep and brought you back to base camp. Doc checked you over and patched you up. You got some stitches in your nose."

Andy reaches up and gingerly touches himself. It feels as if a potato has been grafted onto his face. The stitches are hard and bristly, and a deep ache radiates from them in response to his touch. It is all starting to come back to him: the confrontation with the bespectacled soldier, the listless coupling with Lee. Something happened after he left the Houston Bar and went to find the others. He cannot quite recall what; it is dangling just beyond his reach.

"Doc says you're fit for duty, which is good, because I volunteered us to go on a mission tomorrow."

"You did what?"

"I was over at the CP getting mail when a captain from Civil Affairs came in looking for a squad of grunts to go on a mission to relocate montagnards living in the free-fire zone. I told him I'd do it, and that I'd get some other guys to come along."

"Horvath, are you nuts?"

"Come on, Andy, you've only been in base camp a day, and look what kind of shape you're in. Imagine how you'll be after a week. This is a chance to do something interesting, and maybe even do some good for a change. You know what I mean when I'm talking about 'montagnards?'"

"They're the Vietnamese who live in the highlands; the ones the Special Forces are working with."

"Right, but they ain't actually Vietnamese. They're a different race, more like the natives in Malaysia, and they were here before the Vietnamese. When the Vietnamese came down from China centuries ago, they drove these people into the hills where they've been living ever since. 'Montagnard' is the name given them by French missionaries. It means 'mountain people.' They have a lot of different tribes."

"Kind of like the American Indians."

"Just like them. The montagnards live by hunting and by farming little patches of land that they burn off in the jungle. After a few years, the land gets used up and they move on to another place."

"How did you learn all this?"

"On my in-country R&R, before I got in trouble, I spent a lot of time hanging out with the Green Beanies in Nha Trang. They're a really good bunch of guys. When I get back to the World, I'm going to apply for Special Forces training."

"Hey, what are you, some kind of lifer?"

"Maybe I am. You got to understand, Andy, I ain't like you. I wasn't born in the good ol' U. S. of A. I lost my country to the communists a long time ago. The Army is the best home I've had since then."

"Sorry, man, I understand."

"No sweat. Anyway, the montagnards have never gotten along with the Vietnamese. The Vietnamese don't let them have any rights, and they call them 'moi,' which means 'savage.' So it ain't hard to guess who gets the short end of the stick when it comes to designating free-fire zones. The Vietnamese province chief says, 'Golly, here's the chance I've been waiting for to get rid of those little bastards.' He tells his American counterpart to blow away anything that moves."

"It really is a beautiful war, isn't it?"

"Ain't that the truth. But along comes this Civil Affairs captain, and he says, 'It don't make much sense blowing the shit outta these people who are supposed to be our friends.' He gets the engineers to build a camp out on Highway 19 where the montagnards can live safely. And now he's going out in the boonies to find a village that will agree to relocate. It's like a test case. If he can get one village to get with the program, he figures others will follow."

"How many guys are going on this mission?"

"Just a few Civil Affairs people and a squad of grunts for security. The captain thinks that if we go in with too many people, the montagnards will run away and hide. Bird and Hot Rod are coming. I've signed up Doc Petersen, too, and a couple other guys I know."

"This sounds kind of dangerous to me."

"It won't be too cool if we run into a force of any size. The idea is to get in and get out fast, before Charlie figures out we're there."

"So we'll be risking our necks to save people from our own artillery."

"That's affirmative. I've seen us pulling a lot of really bad shit over here. This is a chance to do one good thing, you know what I mean?"

"I do know what you mean. I remember when the Preacher lit up that farmer in the paddy, and when Dingle Berry told us to drop a frag on those girls in the cellar."

"Life is cheap here, man."

"But why do we do stuff like that?"

"First, because it's often safer to shoot first and ask questions later. Hey, for all we know, that farmer might have been a lookout for Charlie, and the girls in that root cellar might have been out rigging booby traps the night before. Second, for the same reason a dog licks his balls: because he can. One thing you learn here, Andy, is what people will do to other people when the regular rules that we're used to are gone."

"But even here there's right and wrong, isn't there? How can they get away with it? Why do we let them?"

"When a guy's own life ain't worth nothing, it's hard to preach to him about right and wrong. In Nam, we make our own rules, and the biggest rule of all is you don't rat on your buddy. It ain't right what Preacher did, but I owe my life to that dude, and I ain't gonna be the one to turn him in."

"Are they going to stop the bombing and shelling while we're out there?"

"Hah! You're learning. I asked the same question, and the captain said there's gonna be a hold on all arty in the area while we're out there. I noticed you said 'we,' by the way."

"Hey, man, you haven't steered me wrong yet."

*

"Hey, Horvath, are you awake?"

"Yeah, Andy, what is it?"

"I just gotta tell you, man, this sucks."

"Yeah, so what else is new?"

"Why do I let you talk me into this shit?"

"You think you got it bad? Just be glad you ain't Charlie, living in a tunnel with nothing to eat but a rice ball and some *nuoc mam*, hiding from the B-52's until you're told to make a suicide attack against some American position."

"I guess you're right. I wouldn't want to be Charlie. They'll sacrifice ten of him to get one of us, and call it a victory."

"They may be right. Americans don't have much stomach for dying."

"Why should we, if we don't understand what we're dying for?"

"You got a point there, buddy. We'll fight like a bastard when we're cornered, but we ain't looking to mix it up with Charlie. We'd rather let our firepower do the work for us. Sometimes I almost envy the little fucker. He's fighting for his country, and we're just fighting to survive."

*

In the cold of the morning, with the muddy taste of mess hall coffee still in his mouth, Andy continues to have second thoughts about this adventure. Two Hueys sit idling on the dewy Golf Course grass. They will be enough to carry the entire party. The grunts from Third Platoon mill around nervously, talking in low tones. They are not used to going out to the boonies in such a small group. The plan is for them to be gone, with their mission accomplished, before the local VC can learn of their presence and decide what to do about them. As Horvath says, if they get caught by a unit of any size there will be nothing for them to do but "bend over and kiss our ass goodbye." They carry only two days' rations in their packs.

Standing apart from the infantry squad are a scout dog handler and his German Shepherd. Apparently the people they are looking for are so shy that they may have to track them in order to find them.

With a squeal of worn out brakes, a jeep pulls up at the edge of the field, and the captain who is in charge of the mission climbs out. Slight and bespectacled, he has an amiable if somewhat bemused expression. He is accompanied by a slim Viet in custom-tailored fatigues and a wizened little old man who cannot be an inch over four feet tall. Close-cropped white hair covers the head that perches like a basketball atop the old man's tiny body. Dark as a Negro's, his face is wrinkled and grizzled with silver stubble. Dressed in baggy khaki trousers and a new red windbreaker, he looks out of place and uncomfortable in the western-style clothes. His rheumy eyes turn apprehensively to the idling choppers.

"Good morning, men," the captain calls, and the grunts form up in a ragged line to hear what he has to say. "I am Captain Niles, and I want to thank you for volunteering to join us on this mission. I'm sorry I'm late. When our interpreter Mr. Bo—" his gesture indicates the old montagnard- "was dropped off this morning, I was distressed to discover that he doesn't speak a word of English. So I had to go running up to Division HQ and find a Vietnamese interpreter. Mr. Bo will translate the montagnard dialect into Vietnamese, and Mr. Ky here-" the Viet smiles and bows- "will translate from Vietnamese to English.

"Mr. Bo assures me that he knows the location of several montagnard villages on the plateau a few klicks south of Route 19. He has agreed to act as our guide. We have identified a landing zone at grid coordinates 354 402, and expect to be inserted there in half an hour. We plan to locate a group of friendly montagnards, and, if all goes well, to extract both them and ourselves tomorrow morning. You men are experienced, and I know I don't need to tell you that we want to move quietly and avoid attracting attention to ourselves. Now, does anyone have any questions? No? Good. Let's go ahead and load on the choppers, infantry squad on the first ship, dog and handler on the second ship with me and the interpreters. Let's go, gentlemen. Good luck, and good hunting!"

"Where did they find that guy?" Andy shouts, as they settle into the slick's cargo bay. "He talks just like my high school English teacher!"

"He reminds me of that character you see on television," Horvath yells in reply, "Mr. Peepers!"

The slicks lift off and scoot out of Camp Radcliff at treetop level. Soon they are passing over a fog swept plateau that is one of the most desolate areas in all of Viet Nam. The vegetation is thick, but it is the low, hardy sort of stuff that can survive without much moisture. Even now, at the height of the monsoon season, the color of this wasteland is more brown than green. Certainly no rice would grow here, which is presumably the reason why the Vietnamese have abandoned the area to the montagnards.

Swooping down over a small clearing, the Hueys hover for a few seconds and then take off again. They have executed a false landing, to confuse any VC who may be watching. This process is repeated two more times before the door gunner signals that they are coming into the true LZ.

It is not much of a clearing, and it looks awfully far down, but the men on either side of him are pushing off the skids, and he can feel pressure on his back as someone behind him tries to get into the door. What the hell, he thinks, and jumps. A large bush rushes up to meet him, and he comes to a rather painful stop entwined in its prickly embrace. *Those pilots*, he thinks, *must stay awake nights thinking up new places to kick people out of their choppers.* He manages to disentangle himself, adding several new scratches to an already impressive collection in the process, and takes up a position with his weapon pointing outward into the dense thicket.

There is a tremendous crash, followed by thrashing sounds, as someone lands in the same bush that ensnared him. Recognizing the red jacket, he realizes that it is Bo, the montagnard interpreter. The primitive tribesman is getting a rather rude introduction to the wonders of the modern world. Taking hold of the old man's leathery hand, Andy pulls him from the bush. Bo is trembling violently and appears scared half to death. He totters over to a large rock where he sits down, closing his eyes and breathing deeply.

The captain appears, then Ky, the Vietnamese interpreter, and finally the dog handler with his German Shepherd. With the group assembled, Bo declares that he is ready to take them to the nearest village. He leads the way through the forest, and after travelling less than half a klick, they come to a well-worn path. They follow the path in an easterly direction, up hill and down, for more than an hour. Unable to see more than a few feet in any direction, the grunts scan nervously for booby traps and ambushes. The presence of Americans here is unexpected, though, and they do not run into any trouble.

Near the point at which the trail crosses a small stream, they find a crater left by an artillery round. The loose earth in the crater is still smoking, indicating that the round was recently fired. Bird suggests to the captain that he radio their position back to headquarters. The captain replies cheerfully that would be a great idea, if he had a clue as to where they are.

Occasionally there are signs of the inhabitants of the region. Freshly cut bundles of twigs lie alongside the trail which, in its muddier spots, shows the prints of small bare feet. They come upon a hut, a kind of way station, that looks as if it has been occupied recently. Sniffing around the hut, the scout dog becomes very excited and pulls the handler along the trail at a rapid pace. They round a bend in the trail, and a village appears before them, a cluster of rectangular huts built on bamboo stilts. A fire is burning, and there are people squatting around it, talking and engaging in various activities. Seeing the German Shepherd approaching, the people come to an immediate and unanimous decision. They drop what they are doing, jump up and run away into the forest, leaving only a scattering of vegetables and basket work lying on the ground.

The captain produces a bullhorn which he holds for Bo, and the old man exhorts the villagers to come out of the woods. But they either have kept running until they are out of earshot, or they are simply not willing to return while the Americans are there. Deciding that the exercise is hopeless, Captain Niles tells the men to leave some rice and cans of milk to show the people that they mean well. If they are unsuccessful in finding another village, they may return and try again here tomorrow.

They move out again on the main trail. Bo remembers a small village a few kilometers to the east, but is not sure whether or not it is still inhabited. The members of the little group plod wearily along, discouraged to have botched their opportunity for a speedy completion of their mission. The path becomes narrower and less-used. There is nothing to be seen but an unchanging wall of bush.

With the coming of twilight, they still have not found what they seek. Andy is on point, and Horvath is walking slack behind him, when they come to a fork branching off the main trail. Looking back over his shoulder he sees that the German Shepherd, now placed safely at the rear, is straining at its leash. He looks questioningly at the handler, who nods that it is worth checking. Signaling for the rest of the column to stay put and Horvath to accompany him, Andy moves quietly along the path up a gentle rise. A pungent odor tickles his nostrils.

"Do you smell that?" he whispers. "It smells like wood smoke."

Yeah," replies Horvath, "and look how this area is thinning out."

Ahead of them the thick bushes have been cleared, leaving a covering of gnarled and stunted trees. Creeping forward a bit farther, they hear the sound of voices. At this they return to the main trail and report their discovery to the captain.

Excited by the news, Captain Niles announces that this time he is going to take no chances of scaring the people away. He will go into the village with only the two interpreters accompanying him. Andy is somewhat miffed, as he considers the village to be his discovery, but he knows better than to argue with a captain. As the three men disappear up the trail, he sits down with the others to wait.

Half an hour later, Mr. Ky rejoins them, all smiles.

"Kep-tin say come."

Eagerly the remainder of the group follows Ky up the trail. They arrive at a cluster of raised houses and a communal fire, where Bo is engaged in animated conversation with an outlandish figure who is presumably the chief of the village. The chief appears to be older, even, than Bo, and little of his withered brown body is left to the imagination, as he is dressed only in a brief loin cloth. Heavy brass earrings dangle from his earlobes, and his skinny arms are adorned by dozens of brass bracelets. His greasy gray hair is drawn back into a bun and secured by a sliver of bone. He wears another bone ornament in his flat nose. His bright button eyes are fixed on the captain, even though Bo is the one who is doing the talking. His lips are pursed about one of the cigars that the captain has brought along as presents.

Andy notices then that everyone in the crowd of women and children who have gathered to observe the meeting is smoking. No one has been left out. The women are smoking cigars, and the children, down to the smallest toddlers, are puffing happily on cigarettes. It is a scene right out of National Geographic, complete with native women with bare boobs. Some of the younger ones are actually quite comely.

The infantrymen and the children find one another immediately. Candy, chewing gum and cigarettes are handed out. Piggyback rides are given. The captain puts a stop to all the fun.

"Sergeant," he snaps to Bird Lawler, "get your men into some kind of perimeter. Runners have gone to find the people who are out hunting or working in the forest. It won't be long before everyone within ten miles knows we're here, and I'm afraid that includes the VC. Tell your guys to keep their eyes open and not relax for a minute."

While the other men move off to take up positions around the edge of the village, Andy manages to stay close by to listen in on the pow-wow that is occurring between Captain Niles and the chief. The old montagnard is surprisingly receptive to the resettlement proposal, asking few questions and nodding appreciatively as the captain describes the benefits of living under government protection. Even though the montagnards are nomadic, and used to pulling up their roots, the chief must know that the captain's plan would mean a drastic change in his people's way of life. He must have, Andy thinks, a strong reason for wanting to get away, a bigger one than an occasional American artillery round.

On all sides, the people whom the runners have located begin filtering back into the village. Although they supposedly have been hunting and gathering firewood, most of them carry no weapons or burdens of any kind, and Andy guesses that they fled upon learning of the approach of the Americans. They probably did the same thing when the VC came to their village.

The men take places around the fire, while the women hang back with the other onlookers. They vary greatly in appearance, and Andy speculates about the personalities behind the different faces. There are dull faces, sharp faces, cheerful faces and sour. Some of them look like thinkers, others like killers. Although none of these wiry little individuals stands as tall as five feet, their fierce countenances make Andy shiver. He resolves that either he or Horvath will be awake at all times tonight.

After making sure that each new arrival has received a cigar, Captain Niles sits back and waits while the chief describes the proposed plan to the circle of people around the fire. When the explanation is finished, a vigorous discussion ensues. It is obvious that some of the men are in favor of accepting the captain's offer, while others are violently opposed. The climax of the meeting is reached when three of the fiercest looking men rise, stare malevolently at the captain, and stalk off into the forest.

With the air of a statesman, the chief addresses Captain Niles. It has been decided, he says, to accept the captain's proposal. He has given each man the choice of coming along or moving with his family to another village. All but the three who left have agreed to come. The captain makes a short speech, saying that the chief's decision is a wise one that will be of lasting benefit to his people. He says that they must now hurry to gather their things together, for the big bird will be coming to take them to their new homes the very next morning. Then he reaches into his knapsack for more cigars.

The decision having been made, the tension surrounding the meeting evaporates. The people disperse and begin packing their belongings. The chief announces that there will be a celebration in the evening to which all of the visitors are invited.

It is getting late, and so Andy and Horvath dig a shallow hole and construct a roof with their ponchos to shelter them for the night. They build a small fire and heat up a C-ration meal. They cannot see the sun going down, due to the thickness of the forest, but by the time they have finished eating, darkness is gathering in the village. They make coffee from their C-ration packets and relax, sipping and smoking cigarettes. All through the village fires are being kindled. The smell of cooking meat fills the air. Horvath suggests that they take a look around, but Andy is tired and tells him to go ahead without him.

Andy drifts into a semi-doze. When Horvath returns to rouse him, he is surprised to see that his watch reads past nine o'clock. A large fire is burning at the center of the village, and he hears sounds of laughter and shouting voices.

"You've got to come now," Horvath insists. "This is too good to miss."

He follows Horvath toward the glow of the fire. The scene that greets him when they arrive is totally unexpected. All of the villagers, men, women and children, are falling down drunk. The apparent source of their condition is a large clay jar capped with leaves, which has a long straw sticking from it. The montagnards are making periodic trips to the jar and taking drinks through the straw. Several of the Americans are present, and none of them appears intoxicated. Andy is thinking that this is to their credit, when a pretty girl takes his hand and leads him to the jug. He sips tentatively, and it is all he can do to hold down his supper. The stuff smells and tastes like Limburger cheese. Fixing his lips in a polite smile, he sets aside the straw.

"You'll have to do better than that, soldier," Captain Niles calls to him. "If you don't take a good long drink, they're insulted."

Bravely, Andy takes up the straw again. He purses his lips around it, pretending to drink, and as he pulls away fills his mouth once more. He swallows, smacks his lips loudly, and wipes his mouth on the back of his sleeve. The montagnards shout their appreciation.

"What the hell is that stuff?" Andy whispers to Horvath as they move away from the jug. "It's terrible!"

"Trust me, you don't want to know."

"Goddamnit, will you just tell me?"

"It's a kind of rice wine. The captain says the old women sit around and chew up rice and spit it in that jar. When the jar is half full, they pour in some water, cover it with leaves and let it ferment. After a month or so, it's ready. They just stick a straw in and drink it. When it runs out, they pour in more water and it comes out almost as good as before. They've poured in water twice tonight already, and you can see it's still pretty potent."

"Oh, Christ," moans Andy, "I wish you hadn't told me. I think I'm going to be sick. Give me a cigarette."

Horvath lights a cigarette and hands it to him. After a few puffs,

Andy's mouth tastes a little better.

"Captain says getting drunk is part of the 'yards' way of life," Horvath explains. "They do this all the time, the whole village getting smashed together. To them, smoking and drinking are about the most important things there are. They got a real strict moral code, though. They won't steal. And God help you if you mess with their women."

"I'm glad you told me. I think that little gal over there is giving me the eye."

They return to their poncho shelter, and Andy says he will take the first watch. Horvath rolls up in his poncho liner and speaks no more. Andy sits with his back propped against a tree, his rifle in his lap. The night is moonless, and the darkness is intense. The noise of the celebration dwindles into silence, and the cooking fires are reduced to patches of red embers. Remembering the three men who disagreed with the chief's decision, he wishes that Captain Niles had taken the precaution of keeping everyone in the village until their departure.

He touches the bulge that Joan Munson's letter makes in his breast pocket, considers lighting a match to read it, but knows better than to take the risk. He knows it by heart, anyway.

I didn't realize how much I cared about you....

A sweet ache fills his chest, as he imagines Joan sitting at the little writing desk in her bedroom, composing the letter. What would a life with her be like? He conjures up a fantasy of a house with a car in the driveway, a dog, kids, of lying with her in his arms, talking late into the night. A life, just a normal life, looks mighty damn good right now. He has had enough excitement to last a lifetime.

*

In the cornfield outside their village, the montagnards wait quietly with their domestic animals beside heaps of their belongings. Occasionally a baby's cry or the flapping of an escaped chicken breaks the stillness, but such disturbances are short-lived. The carnival atmosphere of the night before has vanished. The montagnards do not look unhappy, but have the patient air of people accepting their fate.

The captain calls Bird over to tell him that a Chinook is on the way. He and the interpreters will go with the montagnards to the resettlement area. The grunts will provide security for the airlift and will be picked up by a Huey a few minutes later. He thanks the sergeant for his help and expresses the hope that they will work together again. As they shake hands, the sound of the approaching helicopter reverberates in the distance.

Bird pops a yellow smoke grenade and stands with his arms raised to guide the chopper in. The montagnards crane their necks, and their eyes grow wide, as the vast bulk of the Chinook floats down above the trees. The ship settles on the smoke, engines straining at full RPM, flattening the knee-high cornstalks in its downdraft. The frightened villagers try to block their ears against the deafening roar, and at the same time to protect their eyes from the stinging dust and bits of chaff that fill the air. Baskets, clothes and all sorts of small articles are tumbling across the clearing, and animals and fowl are running in all directions. The ship bumps down to a landing in the midst of this chaos. The noise of its engines and the wind from its rotors subside. With a mechanical whine, the rear ramp swings down. The mouths of the crew drop open when they see what they have come to pick up.

Captain Niles and the interpreters are motioning frantically for the villagers to move up the ramp and into the helicopter, but the people are having none of it. They are bent on retrieving their animals and belongings that have been scattered far and wide. With the infantrymen and helicopter crew pitching in, they somehow get most of the chickens, ducks, pigs, donkeys, goats, and all of the families save one loaded onto the aircraft. The head of that family gets cold feet at the last moment, does an about-face and leads his wife and children back toward the village. As the ramp swings up, Andy catches a final glimpse of the chief standing in the midst of his people. The grunts are waving, and a few of the montagnard children are bravely waving back. Dust flys again, as the huge ship rises haltingly above the clearing. Reaching a safe altitude, it tilts forward and lumbers off above the trees.

Watching the ship growing smaller, Andy experiences a jumble of mixed feelings as the enormity of what they have done here sinks in. They may have saved the montagnards; or they may have destroyed them. Only one thing is certain: the lives of those people have been forever changed.

The popping of small arms fire puts an abrupt end to his philosophizing. Less than two hundred meters from their position, someone has opened up on the departing chopper. The infantrymen drop to the ground in unison. They show excellent discipline. Not a single man has fired.

"Stay down," Bird calls hoarsely, "and stay quiet! Charlie thinks

115

everybody went on the shit-hook. He don't know we're still here."

The radio crackles, and the voice of the Huey pilot comes over the speaker.

"Slashing Tiger Six-Bravo, this is Apache Two-Two inbound your location. Is your Lima-Zulu secure, over?"

"This is Tiger Six-Bravo," Bird replies. "We are secure, but be advised there are bad guys to our north and the landing zone may be hot. Advise approach from the east and departure to the west, over."

"Roger that, Six-Bravo. Can you pop some smoke for us?"

Bird pulls the pin on a smoke grenade and tosses it into the field. A cloud of thick crimson gushes from the can and spreads out among the cornstalks.

"I see red smoke," the pilot reports.

"That's a rog," Bird replies.

The slick comes in low and fast, its door gunners sweeping the underbrush on either side with their M-60's. There is not even time for the skids to touch down before the grunts are all aboard, falling on top of one another in a jumbled heap. Lying at the bottom of the pile, pressed down by the weight of several bodies, Andy closes his eyes and prays to be lucky one more time.

VIII. LZ SCHUELLER

Snake has departed on the Freedom Bird, slipping away without even saying goodbye. Jason Ash has DEROS'd as well, having his tour cut short after being bitten by a centipede. The Preacher had many enemies, and, although there will never be any proof, Andy suspects that it was no accident that the poisonous insect somehow found its way into the man's bedding. The Preacher's marksmanship will be missed, but Andy is not sorry that he is gone. After being identified as the spawn of Satan, he always had to watch his back when the guy was around. *Look out, America, the Preacher's coming!*

In their place, the Army has provided two new men. PFC Jim Cruikshank is pale and very thin, with a prominent Adams apple and arms that look as if they were squeezed from a toothpaste tube. He is hopelessly uncoordinated, and when he walks, it looks as if he is trying to go in two different directions simultaneously. With red eyes smoldering in a face the color of anthracite, PFC Willie Biggs is built like an NFL tight end; but in spite of his bulk, he moves with the fluid grace of a panther.

They meet the new men while riding in the supply truck to LZ Schueller, a firebase located out on Highway 19 west of An Khe, where their platoon, along with the First Platoon, has been assigned to provide perimeter guard for a 105-millimeter howitzer battery. Squeezed in among stacks of wooden boxes containing artillery rounds, sacks of mail and cardboard crates of C-rations, they gaze out the rear of the deuce-and-a-half. Occasionally they pass bridges and checkpoints

117

guarded by ARVN who look like mushrooms with oversized GI helmets capping slim bodies in tightly tailored fatigues. Most of the time
there is nothing to see but the ribbon of paved roadway unraveling
behind them.

Biggs is composed. He has the look of a veteran already as he
sits holding his weapon, the M-16 like a toy in his big square hands.
Cruikshank is nervous, fidgeting constantly, his eyes rolling as he peers
about for signs of the enemy. He also talks incessantly, asking questions like an annoying five-year-old. He asks where are they going,
what will they be doing, what the platoon leader is like, where will
they sleep, will there be hot chow? Horvath answers the questions
with consummate patience. Andy simply tunes the asshole out, until
it becomes clear that he is being addressed directly.

"What's that on your helmet?" Cruikshank asks. "What does it
mean?"

"Nothing," Andy grunts. "It don't mean nothing."

"Aw, he's just being modest," Horvath puts in. "That's a target
he's got on his helmet. If you look at it close, you'll see it's got a hole
right through the bullseye. Last month we got 'bushed over on the
coastal plain, and this guy took a round dead center in his helmet. It
went in and it went around the inside of his helmet and came out the
back. And it never even touched him. That's why we call him 'Target,'
'cause he can get a hole shot through him and, like he says, it don't
mean a goddamn thing."

"You gotta be kiddin' me!"

"I kid you not, cherry. Our man here is fuckin' invincible. Show
him the hole in the back, Target."

Playing along, Andy takes off his helmet and pokes his finger
through the exit hole, wiggling it around for effect. Cruikshank's eyes
go wide, and even Biggs looks moderately impressed. "Target" is not a
bad nickname, and he is not unhappy at the realization that someone
else will be answering to "cherry" from now on.

Named after an artillery lieutenant who was killed in a plane
crash, LZ Schueller has been occupied by the artillery since soon after
the Cav's arrival in Viet Nam, and there has been ample time for the
cannoncockers to improve the position. The howitzer pits and ammo
bunkers are sandbagged, and the CP, XO Post and Fire Direction Center are all housed in well-fortified structures. The perimeter is surrounded by a deep trench and a cleared area fenced with barbed wire.

When Andy, Horvath and the two replacements dismount the

truck and go in search of the rest of their platoon, Andy remarks that the place looks very secure. Horvath is not impressed.

"They're like sittin' ducks here," he says. "When we're out in the boonies, we never set up in the same place more than a couple a nights in a row. Chuck must know the location of every weapon here, and two platoons ain't much to defend a place like this. Course, we got the cannoncockers too, but who knows how they'll fight. This place is gonna get hit, I guaran-fuckin'-tee it. It's not a question of 'if,' it's a question of 'when.'"

"But we're only eight klicks from Camp Radcliff. Anyone who attacks us here will have the whole First Cav down on him in minutes."

"Charlie ain't stupid. He knows that the Cav moves by chopper. When the weather is socked in, there's only one way to get here, and that's the way we just came, by road. You know, it was just a little way down the road from here that a French mechanized infantry column got ambushed by the Vietminh. You can still see the old burned out tracked vehicles. Those guys got slaughtered, and so did the relief column that came out of An Khe to try to save them."

*

Duty at LZ Schueller is boring, but in Nam, boredom is not such a bad thing. They are on fifty percent alert at all times, but as there is no walking to be done during the day, there is always plenty of time for rest. Only the H&I firing, sporadic during the day and regular as clockwork throughout the night, serves to remind them that there is a war going on. When the rain lets up, there are volleyball games with the artillerymen. The rest of the time, they play cards or cribbage, write letters home, read paperback novels and take care of their equipment. The days pass slowly, but quietly, and it is easy for them to start feeling as secure as if they were in base camp. With a month of his tour gone, Andy decides to start a short-timer's calendar.

One day, a truck driver delivering C-rats and sundries from base camp happens to mention that a montagnard camp has sprung up recently a short distance down the road. Guessing that this must be the very village that they helped to relocate, Horvath becomes very excited. He pesters the lieutenant until Dingle Berry agrees to organize a visit to the camp.

They leave the next morning, as soon as the road has been cleared, in a jeep borrowed from the artillery battery commander. Horvath is driving, and the lieutenant rides shotgun. In the back Andy and Doc Petersen are sitting on a heap of supplies scrounged from the artillery mess hall.

It turns out that the montagnards are living practically next door. In less than five minutes, the jeep is swinging off the highway onto a narrow dirt road. At the corner of the road, a Regional and Popular Forces camp is nestled inside coils of concertina wire. A few uniformed Vietnamese sit up in their hammocks to watch the Americans pass by. On both sides of the road the land has been burned and cultivated in the montagnard fashion. Green shoots are already sprouting in neat rows. On the far side of the clearing, perhaps a half a klick away, several montagnard women are walking in single file, their backs bent under heavy loads of firewood. They plod along in a manner that suggests they have been doing exactly the same thing for the past two thousand years.

The road enters a grove of trees, and the camp comes into view. Andy is surprised to see that the houses have been built on stilts. Except for the sidings of fresh lumber and roofs of corrugated metal, they look just like the houses in the jungle village. This place is clean and free of litter, in stark contrast with the Vietnamese camp outside An Khe, which looks and smells like a garbage dump.

The jeep stops at the center of the camp, and Horvath sounds several beeps from the horn. Children come running from all directions, crowding around the jeep, laughing and holding out their hands.

"Hold your horses, now," calls the lieutenant. "We have to wait for your mommas and poppas before we start giving stuff away."

"Can't we at least give them the chocolate?" Horvath begs.

The lieutenant assents, and Andy breaks open a carton of tropical chocolate bars. Unlike the children of An Khe, who would have been fighting with one another over the candy, the montagnard children wait patiently for their fair shares and smile politely when they receive them. While the candy is being passed out, the old women whose job it is to watch over the children, arrive on the scene. They are soon joined by the wood gathering party and other villagers who come out of their houses to see what the excitement is about.

Andy scans the faces, trying to pick out ones that he can recognize. While some look familiar, he cannot be sure that he has seen any of them before. He only becomes certain that this is indeed the group he and Horvath helped to relocate when the old chief makes his appearance. The crowd parts to clear a way for him, as he walks imperiously to the jeep. Beaming at the Americans, he spreads his arms in a gesture of welcome.

Andy is disappointed that the chief does not appear to recognize him, but is not really surprised. He was only a background player in the resettlement operation, and to a montagnard all the American soldiers probably looked pretty much the same. Rummaging through the sacks and cartons for something special, he settles upon an item which he polishes on his sleeve and presents to the chief with a flourish. The old man accepts the gift and turns it over in his hands, regarding it somewhat dubiously.

"Better explain to him that it's something to eat," Horvath says with a chuckle. "I don't believe he's ever seen an apple before."

"Why don't I just show him?"

Grabbing another apple from the open crate, Andy takes a huge, crunching bite. The chief gets the idea, and bites into his own apple. He chews tentatively, and a smile lights up his wrinkled face. He lifts up the apple and calls out excitedly to the villagers. Soon the Americans are working feverishly to put an apple into every outstretched palm.

Andy finishes his own apple, and is about to throw the core away, when inspiration strikes. Holding up the core so that the chief can see what he is doing, he carefully extracts the seeds and places them on his palm. He pantomimes planting the seeds and young plants sprouting up. The chief nods his understanding and again calls instructions to his people. The apple seeds will not be wasted.

Doc Petersen dispenses medicines and treats the villagers' aches and pains, while the others pass out the rest of the supplies that they have brought. After Dingle Berry shares a ceremonial cigarette with the chief, one head man to another, the Americans depart the resettlement camp, leaving a bunch of happy campers behind them.

"That was a good idea you had, Cullen," Lieutenant Berry says as they speed back along the highway toward LZ Schueller. "Do you think it will work? Will they actually be able to grow apples from those seeds?"

"I don't see why not, sir. My kid sister planted the seeds from an apple she ate once, and a plant came up. It might have grown up to be a tree, if I hadn't accidentally cut it down with the lawnmower."

"If anybody can do it, those 'yards can," Horvath puts in enthusiastically. "Did you see how much planting they've already done here?"

"You're right," says the lieutenant. I wonder why the Vietnamese refugees don't plant anything around their settlements. Most of them are farmers."

"Same reason they let their living areas turn into slums," says Horvath. "Home is where they come from, and all they think about is getting back there. They'll invest their life savings in Coca Cola to sell to the GI's at fifty cents a bottle, or sell their daughters to the brothels in Sin City, but they won't spend a penny to improve their hooches. For the montagnards, home is where they are. They're used to moving around, and scratching out a living in hard places."

"Wouldn't it be something," says Andy, "if we come back twenty years from now and find a grove of apple trees?"

"Yeah, Mr. Appleseed, that would surely be something. I'll tell you what, though, I'll just be happy if there are still montagnards here in twenty years. Those Ruffs and Puffs are supposed to be protecting them, but they could also be here to keep them in, kinda like a concentration camp, you know?"

"As long as Uncle Sam has anything to say about it," the lieutenant puts in complacently, "they've got nothing to worry about."

*

No one notices when Andy enters the smoke-filled dugout. The men sitting beneath a flashlight dangling from a cord are intent on the card game in progress. Hot Rod and a couple of cannoncockers are waiting with folded hands, as Bird Lawler deals to Horvath, a red-haired artillery sergeant and himself.

"Last card, gentlemen, down and dirty."

The cards snap down crisply, and there is a pause, while the players evaluate what their luck has brought them. Bird nods to the artillery sergeant.

"Still your cowboys, Sar'nt."

The sergeant has two kings showing, and an ace. With a confident smirk, he drops two bills onto the heap of military payment certificates on the table.

"Twenty."

"Too rich for me," says Bird, turning over his cards. "How about you, Horvath?"

Horvath also has a pair showing, but they are deuces. Beyond that, his cards show nothing special. With a bored expression, he shoves a bunch of MPC's into the center of the table.

"He raised," says Bird, making no effort to conceal his surprise.

Bird is counting the money that Horvath has added to the pot.

"Thirty-five," he announces. "Cost you fifteen to play, Sar'nt."

Pulling on his lower lip, the artillery sergeant reexamines his hole cards.

"Yer bluffin'," he concludes. "I'm jist gonna have to raise you back." He wets his thumb to peel bills off a fat roll. "Yer fifteen... an' thirty more."

Horvath hardly misses a beat in shoving more MPC's into the pot.

"Fifty," Bird announces. "He raised you twenty, Sar'nt."

The artillery sergeant tugs at his earlobe, then uses a finger to explore the interior of his nose.

"Think you can bluff me, kid, yer crazy. Back fifty!"

"We've already had three raises," Bird says apologetically. "That's the limit."

"Let him decide," the sergeant snarls.

Without hesitation, Horvath tosses in his money. The artillery sergeant recoils as if slapped.

"Well now," Hot Rod drawls, "it looks like Horvath wasn't bluffing."

"He calls," Bird announces. "The pot is right. We'll see you, Sar'nt."

The sergeant is squirming noticeably in his seat, and his eyes have shifted away from Horvath, as he turns over his hole cards.

"Two pair!" exclaims Hot Rod, as the ace appears. "He's got you, sarge. C'mon, Horvath, show us that third deuce."

Horvath makes no move to expose his hand. He sits back comfortably, a smile playing on his lips.

"Goddamnit, soldier, I paid to see 'em!"

The sergeant reaches out and turns over Horvath's hole cards. There is a moment of stunned silence, as all present stare in disbelief at the cards lying face-up on the table. Horvath has nothing- nothing other than the pair of deuces that were showing.

"Horvath," Hot Rod cries in dismay, "why did you call? I can understand why you raised, but why did you call? You were beaten on the board!"

Horvath is rocking back and forth, his mouth emitting an odd wheezing sound.

"He's laughing," says Bird, his face lighting up with understanding. "Don't you get it, Hot Rod? The crazy sumbitch did it as a joke. And he got you, Sar'nt, didn't he? He really got you!"

"Pretty expensive joke," the sergeant grumbles, reaching to rake in the pot.

"Let's go, Hot Rod," says Horvath. "It's your deal. Deal the cards."

*

The artillerymen are doing what they do best, creating a lot of noise and fire and smoke. All six howitzers are firing, the gun crews humping rounds from the ammo bunkers as fast as they can carry them. An actual fire mission is a rarity at LZ Schueller. When Horvath asks one of the gun bunnies what the shooting is all about, he is told that an observer up in a Cessna O-1 Bird Dog has spotted some hooches in the jungle about five klicks to the south that look like a Viet Cong base camp. Shouting a curse, Horvath makes a beeline for the fire direction center.

Andy trails after him, shouting at him to stop. They have been told in no uncertain terms that the areas where the artillery operations are conducted are off limits to them. Horvath ignores him, and barges into the bunker. Reluctantly, Andy follows him.

The bunker is windowless, but its interior is well lit by a series of bare bulbs strung across the ceiling. A bank of radios and a field telephone occupy the rear wall. On the left side is a large map of Binh Dinh Province, and on the right a pair of cots placed end to end. Three men, a lieutenant, a sergeant and a Spec. Four, are standing at a chart table in the center of the room. A fourth man, a private, is seated next to the radios. On the table are a chart divided into grids, a large metal protractor, a three-sided white ruler and something that looks like a slide rule, as well as a yellow-bound field manual open to a table of densely spaced figures. The denizens of the bunker are pale as ghosts, troglodytes who never see the light of day. They look like priests of some strange cult, wielding arcane instruments and texts to come up with the data that will cause the rounds to fly through the air and land magically at the desired location. They all freeze in the midst of what they are doing and stare open-mouthed at the intruders.

Horvath strides over to the wall map and traces a path with his finger to a red pin that is sticking up to mark a location.

"Is this your target?"

"That is none of your business," the lieutenant sputters. "What are you doing here? Get the hell out of my FDC!"

"It is my business," Horvath retorts, jabbing his finger at the pin, "because Private Cullen here and me were at this location with a Civil Affairs team just a couple weeks ago. This target of yours is a montagnard village. They're civilians who just want to live their lives without anybody bothering them."

"Now, look," says the lieutenant in the tone of a psychiatrist trying to soothe a dangerously disturbed patient, "I don't make the rules. It isn't my job to determine whether a target is hostile or friendly. That determination is made by our battalion S-3. But I happen to know that the whole area to our south is a free-fire zone, and all activity and structures are to be considered hostile."

At this point, the radio squawks and the voice of the air observer fills the bunker.

"Shining Star Six-Three, this is Star Six-Niner. Did you roger my last correction, over?"

The artillery lieutenant snatches the handset from his RTO.

"Yes, Six-Niner, we roger. Left five-zero, drop one hundred, repeat fire for effect, wait...." To Horvath he says, "Get out now, and I'll forget this ever happened."

Horvath's response is to charge forward and overturn the chart table. Grease pencils, manuals and instruments are scattered in all directions. After a moment of frozen shock, the horrified FDC personnel fall to their hands and knees and scramble to retrieve them. The lieutenant is screaming and reaching for a pistol that is in a holster hanging on the wall. Andy grabs Horvath's arm and drags him from the bunker.

"Oh, man, you've really done it this time!"

"They ran when they saw the dog," Horvath says, "I hope to hell they're running now."

*

"Target, Target, wake up!"

Jim Cruikshank's voice is whispering urgently in his ear. The two of them are sitting in a hole fifty meters beyond the clearing outside the perimeter. The listening post has been established on the orders of

Captain Roth, who apparently agrees with Horvath's assessment that LZ Schueller is a prime candidate for a VC attack.

Horvath himself has been banished from the firebase, returned in disgrace to base camp. For his part in the invasion of the FDC, Andy's services have been donated to the artillery mess hall for KP during the days, and his nights are spent manning the LP. As this is more than his fair share of an indisputably dangerous duty, he sometimes suspects that Dingle Berry is trying to kill him. Now he shakes his head and rubs his eyes and tries to focus on what Cruikshank is trying to tell him.

"What's the problem, cherry?"

"I've been seeing movement out there, lots of movement!"

The night is foggy, and mist is swirling amid the brush and scraggly trees. His first thought is that Cruikshank is seeing things like any normal FNG.

"Take it easy," he says. "When you stare into the dark long enough, your eyes start to play tricks on you. I remember my first night on the Green Line-"

"—Quiet!" Cruikshank hisses. "I'm telling you they're out there!"

The skinny kid is literally shaking with fright. Andy decides to check out the situation for himself. Keeping his eyes unfocused, using his peripheral vision, he lets his gaze wander across the wall of bushes to their front. Fear clutches his heart. The tops of the bushes are moving. When the mist thins for a moment, he glimpses dark shapes moving like wraiths toward the firebase's perimeter. Their silhouettes are broken by clumps of vegetation that have been tied on for camouflage, but there is no mistaking the weapons that they carry in their hands. A twig snaps to their left. A soft voice says something in Vietnamese a few meters to their right. Keying the handset of the PRC-25 that they have with them, he whispers an urgent message.

"Longhorn Two-Six, this is Lima Papa. Be advised you have boocoo Victor Charles approaching your perimeter. Break squelch if you acknowledge. I say again, just break squelch and do not say anything. The fuckers are all around us!"

A series of soft clicks comes from the handset. His warning has been received. Next to him in the hole, PFC Cruikshank is hyperventilating, his breath coming in rasping wheezes so loud Andy fears that the VC will hear them.

"Calm down, Jim," he whispers. "Just cool it, okay? We've done our job, we spotted 'em. Now all we got to do is lay low and stay quiet. It isn't our job to be heroes. Don't fire your weapon unless you really have to, okay?"

From the perimeter comes the sound of a flare gun firing. There is a pop! and the area is suddenly illuminated by the bright white light of a parachute flare. Andy and Cruikshank duck down in their hole, terrified that their position has been revealed. Then they hear, faint but distinct, a metallic punk...punk...punk. It is a sound that Andy recognizes, the sound of projectiles being dropped into a mortar tube. He risks keying his handset again.

"You've got mortars incoming," he whispers. "Get your asses down!"

A tremendous explosion shatters the night. Sappers, Andy guesses, have blown a hole in the wire. Then all hell breaks loose, as all of the weapons on the south side of the perimeter open up and the mortar rounds begin falling inside LZ Schueller. The fire from the American positions is intense. Red tracers are dancing overhead like deadly fireflies. Cruikshank is moaning, but it no longer matters, as the volume of sound is such that he cannot possibly be overheard. Then Cruikshank jumps to his feet.

"We've got to get back!" he screams.

To try to get back inside the perimeter would be suicide, as they would be exposed to friendly and hostile gunfire. He grabs Cruikshank around the waist and is wrestling him down, when there is a blinding flash of light and a concussion that throws him over backwards.

Stunned, he opens his eyes, rubs the dirt from them. Cruikshank is lying heavily upon him. His ears feel as if they have been stuffed with cotton, and the sounds of the firefight now seem to be coming from a great distance. Amid the small arms fire, the crashing of heavy rounds can be heard. Artillery. The blasts are coming all around them, right on top of them. Although the ceiling is too low for ARA gunships to come to their aid from Camp Radcliff, they are well within the range of the artillery there. Andy realizes that the officers within the perimeter have called in fire on the defensive targets.

Jesus Christ! Don't those assholes know we're out here?

The answer comes to him, and it is not encouraging.

They do know, and they don't care. We're on our own.

Overhead, a flare is drifting lazily down on a parachute. In its light he sees that Cruikshank's face is ghastly white, the features slack, the eyes wide and staring. As he pushes the boy's limp body off him, his hand goes deep into a gaping cavity in his chest. His fingers touch the warm and slippery and still fluttering muscle of Cruikshank's heart, and he jerks his hand back in horror and revulsion.

Cruikshank is dead, there is no doubt about that, and he digests that knowledge with a mixture of sorrow and guilty relief. If the kid had been wounded and alive, he would have had to face the dilemma of whether or not to try to bring him in. As it is, there is only one thing for him to do. He lies back in the foxhole, pulling Cruikshank's body over him for concealment.

*

In the morning Andy walks back through the perimeter, carrying Cruikshank over his shoulder. There are several VC bodies in the wire, their limbs stiffened in odd, twisted postures that remind him of roadkill. They are the first enemy KIA's he has actually seen, it having been too dark on the night of the ambush for him to see the PAVN soldier that he was falsely accused of shooting. There are also a couple of dead GI's, laid out in front of the artillery CP and covered with ponchos. He leaves Cruikshank with them.

Dingle Berry comes up to him and takes him by the arm. The lieutenant looks as if he has really been through the wringer, his face filthy and his uniform in tatters. His lips are moving, but Andy cannot hear what he is saying through the ringing in his ears. He indicates by gestures that he is deaf, and the lieutenant pulls a notebook and a pencil from his pocket. Scribbling a brief message, he passes it to Andy.

"Great work! I'm putting you in for a Bronze Star."

Andy shrugs indifferently, and the lieutenant takes the notebook again.

"What happened to Cruikshank?"

Andy takes the notebook and pencil and writes.

"KBA."

The lieutenant shakes his head sadly.

"We won't tell the family that. Or the FO either, for that matter. He was shot by the enemy- that OK with you?"

Well, how about that? Dingle Berry just might not be a complete asshole after all. He takes the pencil from the lieutenant again.

"That's a rog."

IX. DEVIL DOGS
ARE DELICIOUS

Andy is lying on his cot in Third Platoon's hooch. It is mid-morning, but he has not yet made the effort to get up. He will stay where he is as long as his bladder allows. After Doc Petersen made sure that none of the copious amount of blood on him was his own, he was put on a three-quarter-ton truck and driven back to base camp with the other ambulatory wounded. At the field hospital he was given a bottle of Darvon and some cotton for his ears, and a note saying that he was to be excused from duty until his hearing returned. He was then sent back to his company area.

Word of his heroics has gotten around, and he has become something of a celebrity. At the EM Club, where he spends much of his time, it is not necessary for the man who saved LZ Schueller from being overrun, who lay all night under the dead body of his buddy, to buy his own drinks. He takes full advantage of the situation, and the days pass in a blurry alcoholic haze. The nights are more difficult, as Cruikshank keeps appearing in his dreams, ghastly pale, eyes staring, holding his dripping heart in his hands. He wakes every night in the wee hours, drenched with sweat, his own heart pounding.

"The guy died because he panicked," Horvath says, telling him what he already knows. "He was a cherry and he made a stupid cherry mistake. It's the law of the jungle, man, survival of the fit. It don't mean nothing. Forget about it."

Forgetting is easier said than done. The truth is that it is not

Cruikshank's death that worries him; it is his own. He has thrown away his bloody clothes, scrubbed his body until it feels flayed, but he cannot shake the memory of the long night spent cowering in the foxhole, certain the whole time that the very next moment will be his last. He does not believe that he survived because he was "fit." He knows that he could very well be dead, and probably should be. He shares none of this with Horvath, because he is ashamed. All the time he is being hailed as a hero, he is in reality a coward. Although his hearing has almost completely returned, he pretends that he is still deaf, to avoid being sent back to LZ Schueller.

Hearing footsteps entering the barracks, he remains motionless and keeps his eyes closed until he feels a hand fall on his shoulder. It is Horvath, and he is holding a package wrapped in brown paper.

"Mail call," he says, mouthing the words in an exaggerated fashion so that Andy can read his lips, and pointing a finger at the package. "Package from home."

The return address indicates that the package is from his mother. Tearing the paper and opening the box, he finds some brownies in wax paper, a tin of homemade chocolate chip cookies, and six cellophane-wrapped packs of snack cakes.

"Devil Dogs!" he cries. "My favorite! Oh, thank you, Mom! Thankyou-thankyou-thankyou-thankyou!"

"The fuck's a Devil Dog?" Horvath asks.

"You've never had a Devil Dog? Where have you been, man? Here, try one!"

Tearing open a cellophane package, Andy hands one of the cakes to Horvath and keeps the other for himself. He takes a bite and chews slowly, savoring the combination of rich devil's food and sweet crème filling. He closes his eyes, and in that moment everything is swept away, the rain, the mud, the fear and the horror. He is at home.

"Hey, man," says Horvath, "this ain't bad."

"Not bad? Not bad? Devil Dogs are delicious!"

"Okay, okay, they're delicious. Hey, Andy, you're hearing what I'm saying. You can hear me."

Oops, busted.

"Yeah, it's a lot better this morning. You're still coming in kind of faint, if you know what I mean, but yeah, I can hear you."

"Man, that's great! This calls for a celebration. What you say we get ourselves a jeep and go down to Alpha Kilo this afternoon?"

He is hardly in a mood for celebrating, but, thanks to the Devil

Dogs, he does feel somewhat better.

"All right," he replies. "Why the hell not?"

*

The drinks at the New York Bar are generous, and, by stateside standards, inexpensive. They are drinking scotch, Johnnie Walker Black, which Andy is not used to and which has made him even drunker than usual. After the waitress has returned for the fifth time, he is ready to spill his guts, literally as well as figuratively.

"You see, Anton, you see, the thing is, I'm scared. I don't think I can do it anymore."

Horvath eyes him blearily, reaches out and pats him on the arm.

"You'll be okay, buddy. You'll see. It don't mean nothing."

"You don't understand. It was all a mistake. I don't belong here."

"Mistake? You volunteered, man, you didn't want to miss out on this big important thing that was happening."

"You want to know the truth? I was cut from my college basketball team. Christ, it seems like such a little thing now, but then-"

"Wait a minute. You're telling me you signed up because you didn't make some team? You gotta be shittin' me."

"You've got to understand, ever since I was a little kid, basketball was the most important thing in my life. I always dreamed of playing for Syracuse, but by the time I graduated from high school, I knew that wasn't a realistic goal. I went to the local community college, where I thought I'd be sure to get some playing time. It was right in my hometown of Utica, where people knew me. I was actually something of a local celebrity."

"A big jock, eh? What went wrong?"

"Everything went fine at first. I was a starter on the freshman team, and I had a pretty good season. The trouble came in my sophomore year, when I was trying out for the varsity. The coach went out and recruited these two black kids, one from Brooklyn and the other one from the Bronx. I wasn't too happy when those guys showed up, but I never dreamed they'd get me kicked off the team. They were good ball handlers and excellent shooters, but neither one of them was as good a playmaker as I was or worked as hard as I did on defense. I was sure the coach could see this, so I wasn't worried. Then the day came when the roster was posted."

131

"And your name wasn't on it."

"I couldn't believe it! It had to be a mistake! I went and saw the coach. 'Cullen,' he told me, 'you're a good solid high school player, but we need more than that here at Mohawk Valley Community College.' So there I was, a failure at the age of nineteen. Everything I'd dreamed of, everything I'd lived for, was gone. I couldn't face people with them knowing what had happened. The very next morning, I went down to the recruiting station. I gave up my college deferment and volunteered for the infantry."

"Man, that is some story."

"Just about the stupidest goddamn thing you ever heard, right?"

"Oh, I don't know. Sometimes things happen for a reason. When you get back to the World, you can follow your dream again. Who knows, maybe you'll even end up playing for Syracuse."

"Fat fucking chance! All I want right now is to get out of this place. I've lost my nerve."

"It happens to all of us, man. You'll be okay when we get back to the boonies. Like getting back on the horse that kicked you. You and me are gonna go out there and kick some ass."

"What do you mean, 'you and me?' You're short, Horvath. You're out of here in just a few days."

"Well, Andy, I've been thinkin' about that. And you know what I decided? I'm gonna re-up, you know, extend my tour."

"Extend?"

"That's affirm."

"When you have a chance to get out of here and go home? Are you out of your fuckin' mind?"

"Well, you gotta understand, Andy, home for you ain't exactly home for me. I lost my home a long time ago. America is okay, don't get me wrong, but the truth is, I never really fit in there. The Army is my real home. It's where I fit in."

"You? Fit in? The Army?"

"Yeah, man. I know it don't seem like it, but I do. Remember when I told you my plan is to apply for Special Forces training, join the Green Beanies?"

"Sure."

"To do that, I need some rank. Now, the first sergeant and me, we go round and round sometimes, but we got an understanding. He knows I'm really a good soldier. The Top told me if I extend for six months, I'll get command of Third Squad when Bird leaves. I'll get my

Spec. 4 back, and by the time my tour is up, if I keep my nose clean, I'll be a Sergeant E-5, and Fort Bragg, here I come!"

"Anton, I don't know what to say."

"Say you're glad I'm gonna be around to take care a your sorry ass!"

"I am! I am!"

"You and me, Andy, we'll make Third Squad, Third Platoon the best damn squad in the First Air Cav. We'll take them cherries and make *boonierats* out of 'em!"

"I'll drink to that."

"I got a better idea. Let's fuck to it."

"No offense, Anton, but I just don't find you all that attractive."

"Ha ha, very funny. I'm talkin' about chicks, man, chicks."

"You mind going over to the Houston Bar? There's a girl there I've got some unfinished business with."

"Any place they got pussy is fine by me. Lead the way, sport!"

There is a shill outside the Houston Bar carrying a sign and calling out to passersby to try to convince them to come inside.

"Pretty gels! Numbah one live show! Chealeadah! See chealeadah tricks!"

As Andy and Horvath approach the swinging doors, arm in arm to keep one another from falling down, the little fellow gives them a conspiratorial wink. A couple of whores are lounging against the wall just inside the door, but they wave them off and proceed in search of a table. The décor has improved significantly since Andy was last here. The furniture has been upgraded. The walls have been painted with scenes of cowboys and Indians. The strategy of upgrading appears to be working, for the place is crowded. They have a hard time finding a table, and have to be satisfied with one that is far from the spotlit dance floor.

The atmosphere in the barroom is one of expectancy. A group of GI's with an extraordinary collection of empty beer bottles arranged on the table in front of them begin a rhythmic clapping. Apparently the floorshow is about to begin.

Andy scans the faces of the many girls who are present, looking for Lee. At the entrance, at the bar, along the wall beside the jukebox, they are gathered like flocks of brightly plumaged birds. At the tables they smoke cigarettes, titter at the soldiers' jokes, sip from tiny glasses of ersatz liquor. Off in a remote corner, a pretty young thing is snuggled up next to a balding, flabby warrant officer who must be at least in his forties. She looks like Lee, but she is not. As he watches, her free hand slips off the table and disappears from view.

There comes a hum and whine from the cheap sound system, and the scrawk of a needle dropping onto a record. Music starts, the blaring trumpets and pounding beat immediately recognizable as Nancy Sinatra's *These Boots Are Made For Walkin'*. With a spirited cheer, the soldiers greet the group of three dancers who come tripping out onto the dance floor.

They are dressed in halter tops, miniskirts and high-heeled boots. Their Oriental hair is covered by light brown shoulder-length wigs. They perform a heel-and-toe step that is a caricature of country-western dancing, raising their knees high and slapping their thighs, completely out of sync with one another. They are absolutely awful, and no one cares, for they are absolutely gorgeous, every soldier's wet dream. They finish their number and prance off the floor to a thunderous ovation from the satisfied GI's.

Next up is a performer whom Andy remembers as Frenchie, the Eurasian prostitute to whom Snake introduced him on his first visit to Sin City. Her wig is blond, but he has no trouble recognizing her horsey face and statuesque physique. She is dressed as a cheerleader, in a pleated skirt and a tight sweater with the letters "UT" on the front. She comes prancing out to the tune of *Deep in the Heart of Texas*, carrying a pair of pompoms, which she flings to the delirious GI's before stripping off her sweater and unveiling her two greatest assets. The crowd sings along enthusiastically, as she does jumping jacks in time:

The stars at night are big and bright
BOOM-BOOM-BOOM-BOOM!
Deep in the heart o' Texa-a-a-s....

Frenchie performs a series of handsprings that reveal that she is not wearing anything beneath her skirt. The crowd roars its appreciation.

"Well, what do you know," Horvath says, "the situation is definitely improving."

One of the pretty "Boots" dancers is approaching their table, swaying her hips, smiling flirtatiously.

"Allo, Ahn-dee."

Her voice! Andy is utterly shocked, as he realizes that it is Lee's face beneath the heavy rouge and face powder.

"My God!" he exclaims. "What have you done to yourself? I didn't recognize you in that getup. You look like-"

"—Like Nahn-cee Sonata?"

"—Like a whore," Horvath puts in.

For some reason the crass statement sets him off, filling him with a blinding rage. Throwing back his chair, he leaps to his feet and lunges at his friend. Being much the stronger of the two of them, Horvath controls him easily, catching him in a bear hug and pinning his arms to his sides.

"Hey, buddy, calm down. I didn't mean nothin'. Just calm down, okay?"

He can feel that his face is beet red, and he is gasping for breath, but he manages to get himself under control.

"Okay," he says, "okay. Let me go."

"You sure?"

"Yeah, I'm sure. Lee, I think you look like a million dollars. Let me buy you a drink."

Tucking her knees together demurely, Lee scoots into the chair beside him and motions to a waitress.

"Lord," Horvath breathes, "You can take my arms, you can take my legs. You can have my left ball. Just please don't strike me blind!"

Completely nude now, except for a pair of white sneakers with bunny tails, Frenchie is executing a back bend. When her hands reach the floor, she walks them forward and grasps her ankles. Farther she bends, and farther, jackknifing her body backwards at an impossible angle, until the blond wig is positioned directly beneath her luxuriant reddish bush. Quivering with the effort of her exertion, she manages a game approximation of a smile. The crowd goes wild.

"Do you see that?" Horvath exclaims. "That's amazing! Think about the possibilities!"

"You want date with Frenchie?" Lee asks him. "Frenchie numbah one boom-boom."

"Does the Pope shit in the woods? Abso-fuckin'-lutely!"

"Can do, GI."

Lee gets up and hurries off, pushing her way through the bamboo curtain. A minute later she reappears with Frenchie in tow, wearing a dressing down, still sporting her blond wig. She leads Frenchie past the tables full of soldiers clamoring for her to join them, and presents her to a beaming Horvath.

"Buddy, didn't I tell you things were looking up?"

*

Back in her cubicle, Andy and Lee undress and lie down on the bed together. He is feeling exhausted, and she seems to sense this, for she tells him to turn over onto his stomach while she rubs his back.

"You tired, GI? You look numbah ten thousand. Let Lee take care...."

Her hands move to his legs, stroking upward, dipping between his thighs, but the increasingly sensual ministrations fail to excite him. He feels a terrible emptiness inside, and the harder he tries to banish it, the deeper and more terrible it gets. Even when she rolls him over and puts her mouth on him, something he has never experienced before, he remains limp and unaroused.

"No sweat, GI," Lee murmurs. "Is okay. You jus' tired. Go sleep now."

And that is exactly what he does, sinking into a blissful sleep, as her cool and soothing hands slide over him.

*

"Three times," Horvath crows, as they stagger into Third Platoon's hooch together, "three times in half an hour! That chick did things I never thought was possible. Andy, I think I'm in love!"

His friend's enthusiasm is not contagious. In fact, after his own failure to perform, Andy finds it downright annoying. He wants only to lie down on his cot and rest until it is time for the EM Club to open. As he lifts the mosquito netting, he is surprised by an angry hissing sound. A rat is on his bed, the size of a small terrier. It is surrounded by a litter of torn cellophane wrappers. Its red eyes glare at him with ferocity and hate.

My Devil Dogs!

An entrenching tool is the weapon closest to hand. The mosquito netting is shredded, and blood and bits of flesh and fur are spattered everywhere, as he brings it down again and again with uncontrollable fury. Horvath stands by and lets him go at it, until, spent and gasping, he finally lets the tool drop to the floor.

"Good job, man. You really waxed that bugger."

X. SORRY ABOUT THAT

In the Nam, you do not have to go looking for trouble; it will
find you soon enough. Andy and Horvath are enjoying a beer at the
EM Club after a pleasant afternoon of shit-burning, when a sergeant
comes in and announces that two companies of their sister battalion, the Second of the Sixth, are in heavy contact somewhere near the
Cambodian border. When he asks for volunteers to go to their aid,
Horvath is the first man on his feet.

"What are you doing," Andy shouts, trying to drag him back
down onto his chair, "are you crazy?"

"Those guys are in trouble," Horvath says simply. "We got to
go."

"What do you mean, 'we?' I can't do this – I can't!"

"Okay, Andy, you stay here if you want to. I'm going, irregard-
less."

Every reasonable bone in his body tells Andy he should stay right
where he is.

"Damn it, Horvath, aren't you afraid of death?"

"Why should I be afraid of death? Hunh! I am death, at least I
was to probably twenty or thirty good boys whose mothers loved them
just the same as yours loves you."

"You sonofabitch, you're going to get us both killed."

Horvath laughs and slaps him on the back.

"Maybe, but it will take a hundred of them to get the two of us.
Come on, let's get our saddle-up gear."

They keep their equipment ready to go on short notice. All they

137

have to do is fill their canteens and draw some grenades and ammo from supply. In fifteen minutes they are in the back of a deuce-and-a-half with others from their unit who have been cajoled or coerced into volunteering: a motor pool mechanic, a cook, and the two headquarters clerks, as well as their regular medic, Doc Petersen, who happened to be in base camp collecting medical supplies for LZ Schueller.

"I can't believe we're going into combat with these REMF's," Andy declares, not caring that the objects of his scorn are there to hear him.

"These guys will be fine," Horvath asserts. Although outranked, he has been made leader of their ragtag squad by virtue of his superior experience. "Okay, guys, listen up. The LZ we're heading for is gonna be hot. Keep your ass down, and don't shoot unless you know what you're shooting at. Stay close to me and Target, and do what we do, and you'll be okay."

At the Golf Course, a row of slicks is waiting, their turbine engines idling, the rotors slicing the air in lazy whorls. When the trucks are unloaded, a company-sized unit is assembled. The relief force is commanded by a captain from Div Arty and a heavyset senior NCO who looks familiar, but whom Andy cannot place, until the man says to him:

"You step on my toe again, young man, and I'll ream you a new one."

Amazed, he recognizes the first sergeant as the same one who chewed him out on the plane coming over from California, what now seems like a hundred years ago. The effect of this is not reassuring, but rather enhances the already nightmarish quality of the scene. Who will appear next? He half expects to see his friend Ty, or Snake and the Preacher, or even the unfortunate Cruikshank.

The artillery captain, who was a famous football player in his days at West Point, delivers a pep talk to the men standing in formation.

"It's the fourth quarter, and the clock is running down, and we're two touchdowns behind," he tells them, "but men, the game is not over. We're better than Charlie, and do you know why? We've got a deeper bench, that's why! We're going to turn this game around."

"Win one for the Gipper," an anonymous voice mutters quietly but clearly from the ranks.

The captain's face twitches, and then goes blank, as he decides to pretend that he has not heard. He waves his arm in a signal to load on the choppers.

"Come on," he cries, "let's get out there and kick some ass!"

They board the second slick in line. Andy is the last to load, so as to be the first one off when they hit the LZ. Sitting with his legs dangling out of the open doorway, he takes a last longing look at Camp Radcliff as they lift off from the Golf Course and follow the ribbon of Highway 19 as it unravels to the west. The terrain below is familiar to him now. He recognizes the ARVN checkpoints and the montagnard relocation camp, and then spots LZ Schueller with its six tiny howitzers resting in circular gun pits.

They cross the mountains at the Mang Yang Pass, and leaving the densely populated area of Pleiku to their north, enter an area where an unbroken canopy of treetops stretches away as far as the eye can see. Half-drunk when he left the EM Club, Andy is now cold sober and wondering how he could have been so foolish as to get himself into this clusterfuck. Ahead of them the burning disc of the sun is hanging beneath a dense cloud cover, flooding the sky with red, and it seems to him that they are flying into a swirling vortex of blood.

Horvath taps him on the shoulder and points toward the horizon. The first thing he sees is the smoke, a dirty smudge spreading over the jungle. Then he spots the fast movers, F-4 Phantoms, tiny specks circling like gnats above the smoke. One of the jets swoops low over the jungle, and as it rises, a bright orange fireball blossoms in its wake. The zoomies are dropping napalm, a sure sign that a sizeable enemy force has been engaged.

As they drop to treetop level and begin their run for the LZ, Andy feels the old familiar exhilaration in spite of himself. A clearing appears, a ragged oval blasted out of the jungle. The scene below is one from hell, marred by bomb craters, with small fires burning and doll-like figures of men scattered over the earth, whether living or dead he cannot tell. The door gunner next to him begins firing, and this is his cue to slide his ass out to the edge of the floor and rest his feet on the skid. Seeing purple smoke gushing amid shattered trees that jut up like giant stalagmites, he wonders how anyone could consider this to be a landing zone.

The pilot is good. He finds a gap in the trees and brings them in a few feet above the ground. As they come to a hover, the ship lurches and its skin is torn by a hail of gunfire. Andy is thrown clear, and the hard landing knocks the wind from his lungs. Lying on his back and gasping for breath, he sees the chopper yawing crazily above him. It has become a death trap, and men are tumbling out like rats deserting a sinking ship. Somehow the pilot manages to regain control, and the chopper escapes with its belly skimming the treetops, pursued by tracers like a swarm of angry green hornets, the door gunner hanging limp in his harness.

The American force occupies a saddle on a north-south ridge line, and the LZ sits atop the southern hump of the saddle. Only the first two choppers of the airlift have made it in. The others have had to abort, due to the heavy groundfire. As the artillery captain is on one of the ships that has turned back, First Sergeant Huddleston, who came in with the squad on the lead chopper, is in command. Taking a headcount, he determines that miraculously all of their little band are alive. A couple of the men have sustained superficial wounds, and these Doc Petersen patches up and declares fit for duty.

With the helicopters gone, all of the firing has ceased. Telling them all to stay put, the first sergeant goes to report to the battalion commander, who is hunkered down in a bomb crater a short distance away. He returns a few minutes later and tells them that the LZ has been under assault by an NVA regiment, and although the enemy has been repulsed for the time being, another attack is likely. Their orders are to provide security for the command post and an aid station that has been set up nearby to care for the wounded. With the front lines more than fifty meters away, they are not to fire unless it is plain that their position is being overrun. Darkness is falling as they establish an inner perimeter and eat a quick meal of cold C-rations.

Horvath and Andy occupy a foxhole that has been conveniently left behind by the Second of the Sixth troopers. As he is far too keyed up to sleep, Andy takes the first watch, standing chest-deep in the hole with a row of grenades laid out along the rim in front of him. The sky continues to be overcast, and the night is so dark, he cannot see his own hand when he lifts it in front of his face. He hears the moaning of the wounded at the aid station, and voices talking on the radio at the CP. The artillery FO is calling in fire on their defensive targets, in order to discourage any enemy who might be closing in under cover of darkness. Soon the rounds begin to fall, whining overhead and smashing into the jungle with bright flashes and jarring concussions.

Typically, Horvath sleeps through it all, wrapped in his poncho liner at the bottom of the hole. Andy no longer marvels at his friend, but he does envy him, as cold snakes of fear writhe in his own entrails. In a nearby foxhole, one of the headquarters clerks is whimpering, calling for his mother. Even as he calls out to the man to be quiet, Andy feels like doing the same. He has a very bad feeling about this place, a sense of foreboding that he cannot shake, no matter how many times he tells himself it is all in his mind.

In the night a cold rain falls, turning the already muddy LZ into a quagmire. It is after four o'clock in the morning when, in a dazzling burst of light, the world is ripped asunder and comes together with a clap of thunder. Andy hears the colonel shouting at the FO to have the artillery cease firing, and the FO shouting back that it is not artillery that is incoming, but enemy mortars. All hell is breaking loose, the rounds falling upon their position with deadly accuracy. On it goes, and on, a relentless pounding, filling the air with humming shrapnel and sending up geysers of mud and rocks that come raining down upon them. Cowering in the hole with his eyes closed and his hands covering his ears, Andy sees Cruikshank's ghastly face, feels again his hand going into the boy's chest, and finally he cannot take it anymore. The dam that has been holding back the horror within him bursts, and he begins to scream. He is screaming, screaming, and that is the last thing he remembers when he opens his eyes in the gray light of dawn and sees Horvath looking down at him.

"How are you feeling, buddy?"

Asking himself the same question, he decides that he does not really feel too bad. His head aches, but there is nothing unusual about that, and he has a strange floating sensation, almost as if he has been drugged.

"What the fuck happened?" he asks. "Am I hit?"

"Just by me. You went south on me, buddy, and I had to cold cock you. Gave you my best shot, and you went out like a light."

Horvath holds up his clenched fist to illustrate his point, and Andy realizes that much of the pain in his head is radiating from his jaw. Touching his chin gingerly, he finds a considerable lump there. When he bites down, his teeth do not mesh properly.

"Jesus. How long have I been out?"

"Couple hours. Actually, you were only knocked out for a minute. I'd say you were just sleeping, sleeping like a baby."

"What happened? I mean, the last thing I remember is we were getting mortared."

"Yeah, that kept up for about an hour, and then everything got real quiet. I thought Charlie was going to attack then, but nothing happened."

"All of our guys okay?"

"Yeah, but the aid station took a direct hit. Six of the wounded are KIA, and the others are fucked up pretty bad. The colonel is bullshit because the dust-off choppers won't fly in until the LZ is secure."

"Seems pretty quiet now."

"Yeah, but who knows? Maybe Charlie's dee-deed, but maybe he's still laying in the weeds. We're supposed to take a patrol out the northern end of the perimeter and check things out."

"You're shitting me!"

"I shit you not. The FO's gonna do a recon by fire, and we're gonna follow the rounds. I want you on point, Andy. You gonna be okay?"

"I don't know. I really don't. I cracked, man, cracked wide open."

"Well, I can't put Tweedledee and Tweedledum on point, now, can I?" Horvath is referring to the two headquarters clerks, who are rumored to be a couple. "The other guys ain't much better. Come on, man, get your shit together. They can only kill you once."

"Why doesn't that make me feel all warm and fuzzy?"

"Hey, here's the deal. You walk point, I make the coffee."

They set out in single file, with their squad in the lead. Andy is walking point, and although he is "back on the horse that kicked him," he is still afraid. If it were not for Horvath trailing him as his slack man, he would be tempted to cut and run; but his fear of showing cowardice in front of his buddy is even greater than his fear of dying. As he picks his way through the tangle of splintered stumps and fallen trees, he hears a crackle of small arms fire and the sharp pops! of bullets passing overhead. Acting the point man's part, he swings his weapon to the left and right, but he actually sees nothing. Fear has made his vision as constricted as if he were walking along a tunnel.

After they have walked a little more than fifty meters, they begin to pass Second of the Sixth troopers coming in the opposite direction. Many of them are wounded, with blood-soaked field dressings applied to various parts of their bodies. Those who are unable to walk on their own are aided or carried by their buddies. Haggard and filthy, they pass by with their eyes down, barely giving the fresh troops a glance.

Reaching the edge of the landing zone, they enter a dense undergrowth of leafy plants and bushes taller than a man. Medium-sized trees rise out of the ground vegetation, and above them tower the tops of giant teaks and mahoganies. This is the triple-canopy jungle that Andy has heard of, but has never seen before. The three levels of interlocking branches do not admit much sunlight. Even though it is well into the morning, they are moving through a gloom that is like twilight.

"What the fuck you doin', man? You wanna get zapped? Git yo' ass down!"

The voice sounds right next to him, yet he is unable to see the speaker, until he realizes that what he thought was a bush is staring at him with wide and angry eyes.

"Git down, dumbass! Now!"

As he drops to the ground, there comes a crackling burst from an AK-47. Bits of leaf and twigs rain down on him, as the vegetation is shredded overhead. Horvath crawls up beside him, his rifle cradled on his forearms.

"The fuck's goin' on here?"

"Snipers in the trees," says the trooper, "dat's wha's happenin', man. Who de hell 're you guys?"

"We're from the First of the Sixth," Horvath tells him. "We're here to bail out your sorry asses."

At that moment there comes the fluttering whine of an arriving artillery volley. The rounds crash into the jungle unseen, about a hundred meters ahead.

"The dinks are closer to us than those rounds," says Horvath, "right?"

"Dat's a rog," confirms the trooper. "Dey's close enough to spit at."

Another volley impacts, farther away than the first.

"Shit!" Horvath exclaims. "This is turning into one giant clusterfuck."

There is a thrashing in the underbrush behind them, and First Sergeant Huddleston emerges, walking upright, a .45 pistol in his hand. There are patches of high color on his cheeks, and his square jaw is jutting pugnaciously.

"What are you men doing?" he shouts. "Why have you stopped?"

The trooper groans and covers his helmet with his hands.

"Get down, Top," Horvath says. "The dinks are between us and the arty. Better get the FO on the horn and have him walk the rounds in closer."

"He's not on our net, and I don't have his freq. Our orders are to follow the arty, and it's getting ahead of us."

"Top, with all due respect-"

"Move out, soldier, that's an order!"

This is crazy, thinks Andy, *I should tell that idiot to go fuck himself.* But Horvath is still moving, and as long as Horvath is moving, Andy will too. He crawls ahead, working his way through vines and bushes. The jungle closes him in on him, so close, he cannot see more than three feet in any direction. Random thoughts are flashing through his head, memories of things not accomplished or left undone. He remembers an airplane model that he never finished, an exam failed due to lack of preparation, a basketball game when his team was beaten at the buzzer. An image of Joan Munson floats by, as always, far beyond his reach. He thinks of Lee back in Sin City. Three times he has been with her, and he still has not managed to do it right. A case could even be made that he is still a virgin.

Jesus Christ, Andy, now is not the time to be thinking about sex!

A body is blocking his path. The young GI is lying on his back, staring up at the jungle canopy. Ants are crawling on his face, but he makes no move to brush them away. *Someone ought to get those ants off him,* Andy thinks, but he cannot take the time. He averts his eyes and pushes on.

From somewhere ahead of him a new sound begins, slower and deeper than the AK-47's, a dangerous jackhammer pounding. A Chi-com .51 caliber machine gun is traversing back and forth, probing the underbrush with short, businesslike bursts, searching for victims, searching for him. He ducks behind a tree, and, like magic, the trunk sprouts a neat row of splintered holes inches above his head. The tree might as well be made of papier-maché, for all the protection it provides.

More artillery rounds crash into the jungle, too far away to be of any use. Reluctantly abandoning his cover, Andy wriggles along the ground like a reptile, literally plowing a furrow through the spongy soil. After struggling through the dense underbrush for a distance of perhaps twenty-five meters, he comes to a place where the enemy has cleared fields of fire. On the other side of the clearing is a mound that looks at first like an anthill, but which he recognizes as a bunker. From a dark slit the barrel of the machine gun is protruding, and he can see the muzzle flashes, as it spits death at three thousand feet per second.

Something snaps within him, some circuit reaching overload and blowing a fuse. *Fuck it.* He no longer feels fear, or, for that matter,

144

much of anything else. The only reality is here and now, the air in his lungs and the blood pumping through his veins. Everything seems to be happening in slow motion, and he is able to see the situation with great clarity. Flipping the selector switch to rock 'n' roll, he fires a well-aimed burst at the opening in the bunker. He succeeds only in attracting the gunners' attention. As the air about his head is shattered by a burst of whiplash cracks, he rolls to his left and takes up a new firing position.

Amid the noise of the firefight, he hears shouting. A message is being passed along the line. A voice surprisingly close to him, which sounds like Doc's, calls out:

"ARA comin' in! Everybody throw smoke, don't matter what color!"

Andy also yells, repeating the message for the benefit of anyone within earshot. Although unable to communicate adjustments to the artillery, the first sergeant has apparently succeeded in getting in touch with the helicopter gunships. The GI's are being told to mark their positions with smoke, so that the pilots will know where it is safe for them to fire their rockets. Andy sees clouds of red, yellow and violet smoke seeping up from the underbrush, and prays that the signals will be visible above the topmost layer of canopy. Removing one of the smoke grenades that is hanging on his suspenders, he pulls the pin and hurls it as far as he can out into the clearing.

As he hears the beat of the approaching choppers, he is filled with a savage and bloodthirsty joy. *Die, you motherfuckers!* He exults when, with a great chattering roar, the Huey gunships appear. Then he sees Horvath crawling on top of the machine gun bunker.

Somehow Horvath has managed to circle around and approach the bunker from the rear. His rifle is slung across his back, and he carries a fragmentation grenade in each hand. As he looks up at the Hueys bearing down on him, his face wears an expression of total resignation. There is no time to take cover, no time to run. There is only time to bend over and kiss his ass goodbye.

Rockets streak from the pods mounted on the gunships trailing smoke, and the jungle beyond the clearing erupts in smoke and flame. Andy buries his face in the earth and covers his ears with his hands. When he lifts his head, he sees men coming out of the trees, wearing the light green uniforms and pith helmets of NVA regulars. He picks one at random, and when the man drops to one knee and raises his weapon to fire, aligns his sight picture on his chest and squeezes off a round. The NVA flops over, and he swings his weapon to another target and fires again. This one staggers but keeps coming, and he has to shoot him two more times before he goes down.

Jumping up and running through the brush, he yells for the other members of the patrol to come on line. A few yards away, he finds Tweedledum and Tweedledee huddled together in a depression, their rifles lying on the ground beside them. He kicks them hard in the ass, screaming at them to start shooting, then continues on to rally the others. Many weapons are opening up from their side of the clearing, and the NVA are falling like ducks in a shooting gallery. Andy empties his magazine, reloads and continues firing.

It is over in less than a minute. When the shooting stops, he rises up and cautiously crosses the open space to the bunker. There are no signs of life, but, as Horvath has taught him, a guy can't be too careful. He drops a frag through the firing slit, and ducks to one side as a muffled WHUMP! resounds within. He pokes the muzzle of his M-16 inside and empties an entire magazine. Only then does he go to find his friend.

Horvath is lying facedown on the roof of the bunker. His legs twitch as if shivering, and his back is rising and falling in a regular rhythm. He is breathing!

"MEDIC!" he screams, and Doc Petersen comes running.

Doc turns Horvath over. Unconscious, he is bleeding from the nose, and a peppering of small wounds covers his face and chest. When Doc carefully removes his helmet, it is apparent that blood is coming from his ears as well. But he is definitely alive, drawing in deep, rasping breaths.

"He's got a chance," Doc says. "We've got to get him back to the LZ."

They use a poncho and a pair of saplings to fashion a makeshift stretcher. Doc takes one end and Andy the other, and together they struggle with their limp burden through the dense jungle. Although the assault on the northern side of the perimeter has been repelled, the fighting is not yet over. They still hear firing from a number of locations, and the pop!-pop!-pop! of incoming rounds passing overhead. When they arrive, exhausted, at the aid station, they find that a number of fresh casualties are waiting there.

The truck mechanic, Spec. 4 Don Parisi, is among the wounded, the sleeve of his fatigue jacket torn and bloody and a bandage plastered on his shoulder. A morphine syrette dangles from his arm, and he is smoking a cigarette. When he sees whom they have brought in, his eyes widen in shock.

"Horvath! I don't fuckin' believe it. What the fuck happened?"

"Horvath was trying to take out the Chi-com," Andy explains, "just when the ARA was coming in. He got caught in the target area."

"Fuckin' Huddleston! That goddamn lifer don't know his ass from a hole in the ground."

"It wasn't really his fault," Andy says. "He had no way of knowing Horvath went out there on his own."

"If you say so, man. Hey, they say a dust-off is coming in. We get him on that, he just might make it, hunh, Doc?"

"Maybe," Doc allows. "He's fucked up pretty bad. You just can't tell."

Andy hears the chopper coming, sees the red cross painted on its nose, and the sight fills him with hope. Horvath will make it, somehow he knows it. There is something about the guy that makes him seem indestructible.

The medevac pilot has no desire to try to thread his way among the broken trees. He brings his ship to a hover above the jagged stumps and has his crew chief lower the jungle penetrator, a metal cone equipped with leaves that fold open to serve as seats. Doc Petersen and another medic from the Second of the Sixth let the cone hit the ground to dissipate the static charge, then fold down the leaves. They place one of the slightly wounded men on the seat, then strap Horvath to him, sitting on his lap facing him. At Doc's signal, the crew chief starts the winch, and the cable tightens, taking up the load. The crew chief is guiding the cable with one hand, and the wounded men are thirty feet above the ground, when a burst of automatic weapons fire erupts from the tree line. Looking up, Andy sees the crew chief reach for the cable release on the side of the winch.

"NO!" he screams, but his voice is swallowed up in the general uproar.

When the cable is cut, the sudden release of pressure causes the helicopter to roll over onto its side. The pilot banks sharply left and right to avoid the ground fire, as he guides his ship away from the LZ.

"No!" Andy screams again. "Come back! Cowards!"

He points his rifle in the direction of the departing helicopter and empties the magazine in one long burst. The chopper is well out of range, but he is not aware of that. In his rage, he is actually trying to kill them. Doc Petersen grabs the barrel of his weapon and wrestles it away from him.

"Jesus Christ, Cullen, take it easy! You're losing it!"

He is, indeed, losing it. He has lost it. In one moment he was certain that his friend's life would be saved; in the next, all hope is gone.

Still strapped together, Horvath and the other wounded trooper are lying on the ground a short distance away. The trooper is none the worse for wear, but Horvath is in bad shape, his breathing becoming increasingly labored, consisting now of deep, rattling gasps. Doc does not need to tell Andy that his buddy is dying. Andy is holding his hand, and even though he shows no sign of awareness, is talking to him about their experiences together.

"...Remember that volleyball game we had with the cannon-cockers at LZ English? That guy Lurch was something else! We didn't have a chance against him, not a fucking prayer, but goddamnit, we almost beat him. We almost beat him, you and me and the other guys, because we wouldn't quit. Don't quit now, Anton, hang in there, man, stay with me...."

Horvath stiffens once, twice, three times, then relaxes with a sigh. Doc reaches out and presses fingers to his throat.

"He's gone."

Andy gives his friend's hand a final squeeze and reluctantly lets it go. He feels numb. The magnitude of what has happened has not yet sunk in.

"It wasn't the Top's fault," he says. "He was just following SOP. It wasn't anybody's fault. It was just the luck of the fucking draw. I just wish that medevac crew hadn't of been such cowards."

"I dunno," Doc says. "Maybe it's for the best. He might 've wound up a vegetable if they'd saved him. You know, I'm not even sure the rockets were what killed him. The bleeding from the nose and ears, that's from the blast concussion. But those wounds look to me like grenade fragments, and he might 've got some in his brain. Maybe he took out that bunker just before the ARA strike, and the frags got him through the roof. They don't do autopsies on combat casualties, so we'll never know."

They carry Horvath to a spot where a few other KIA's are lying under ponchos. As they lay him on the ground, his cigarette lighter falls from his pocket. Doc picks it up and hands it to Andy.

"Something to remember him by."

Andy studies the lighter in his hand. It is a cheap Zippo knock-off, the kind sold as souvenirs on the streets of An Khe. On one side is etched a map of Viet Nam with a small star at the location of the Cav's base camp and the year the lighter was acquired, 1965. On the back is engraved a trite GI saying that Andy has heard many times.

> Yea, though I walk through the
> Valley of the shadow of death,
> I will fear no evil,
> For I am the baddest motherfucker in the valley.

Horvath's grenades were not exploded. Only one grenade was used, and that was his own. This realization causes him to feel… nothing. Nothing at all. He pockets the lighter and helps Doc draw the poncho up to cover Horvath's face.

"Sorry 'bout that, buddy," he says.

XI. BADDEST IN THE VALLEY

"Rise and shine, ladies, it's a beautiful day for killing the babies!"

Like pieces of the landscape coming to life, the members of the Third Squad throw off their ponchos and rise to greet the new day. They are good boys, his men, and he feels a paternal protectiveness towards all of them. Willie Biggs, the only seasoned trooper among them, has proven to be a superior soldier, cool under fire with the kind of instinctive understanding of the dynamics of a fight that cannot be taught. The others are all new guys: Eddie ("Pothead") Huggins, a yellow-skinned Negro from Detroit who takes everything, good and bad, with the same laid-back equanimity; Peter Plumb, a "down-eastah" from Maine who possesses the weirdest sense of humor he has ever encountered; Roddy Mattison, a California surfer dude who still cannot believe what has happened to him; and Isaiah ("Ike") McPeak, a country boy from a place so far back in the hills of West Virginia, the news has not reached it that the War Between the States is over. The war has not yet changed them, and they look to him with a trusting devotion that he would find touching, if anything could touch him anymore.

He wanders among them, offering a word of encouragement or advice about their equipment, listening to their complaints and answering their questions as best he can. Outwardly patient and understanding, inwardly he is shocked by their naiveté. They are such a bunch of cherries.

"Hey, Pete," he hears Pothead saying, "do you think it's true what dey say, if Charlie catches you, he cuts yo' balls off an' stuffs 'em in yo' mouf?"

"I don't know, but I do believe that if Chahlie gets his hands on yuh, yuh ahss is grahss and Chahlie is the lawnmowah."

"Cowabunga, daddy," exclaims Roddy Mattison. "It would be a bummer to get shipped back to the World without your balls. What you think they do, throw 'em away, or maybe sew 'em back on?"

"Don't worry about it, Mattison," Pete tells him. "In your case it won't make a bit of difference. Your bahlls are so smahll Chahlie won't be able to find 'em without a microscope."

Andy smiles and moves on. It is time for the mission briefing with Dingle Berry. He joins the other squad leaders at the CP, and the lieutenant fills them in on the plan for the morning.

"The company is going to cordon off the village of Binh Duc, leaving the west side open. Third Platoon will go over the top of Hill 237 and move toward the ville down the east slope. If any VC come out of the village, they should run right into us. We have a lot more ground to cover than the other platoons, so we'll be moving out right away. Tell your men to saddle up."

*

They skirt the edges of the paddies, approaching Hill 237 on the opposite side from the village, and begin their upward climb. The hill is not a large one, but it proves to be a real ball-buster, with a steep slope and ground vegetation that is unusually thick. They go up in single file, with two men on point clearing the way with machetes.

The morning wears on, and as the sun climbs in the sky, the heat becomes unbearable. Andy's fatigues are soaked, and sweat mingled with insect repellent runs stinging into his eyes. His mouth is parched, his tongue filling it like a dead furry rodent. He started the day with only a single canteen of water, and he has been using it sparingly, conserving it as best he can.

The column is spreading out, as the new men have trouble keeping up the pace. Directly ahead of Andy, PFC Roddy Mattison is hurting. He is sucking wind, and his knees tremble with every step. When a low-hanging vine gets caught on the top of his rucksack he does not stop, but presses on, trying to break through it. Andy sees that it is a "wait-a-minute" vine, studded with thorns, and that the thorns have become lodged in the nylon material of Mattison's pack. The vine does not break, and its pressure gradually increases until Mattison cannot move ahead any farther. He struggles to get out of his rucksack, but the straps are now too tight. At last he flops onto the ground, too exhausted to move.

"Easy, buddy, take it easy."

Andy's words are kind, but in his heart he is very angry. The last thing he needs right now is to have this cherry crap out on him. Taking out his knife, he cuts the offending vine. He rolls Mattison over, and is not pleased by what he sees. The young man's face is ghastly pale, and his eyes are dull and unfocused. Andy removes his helmet and feels his forehead. Burning up. He calls ahead to stop the column, and Willie Biggs comes back to help.

"Heat exhaustion," Andy tells him. "We'll have to divide up his load."

Biggs takes Roddy Mattison's pack. Andy takes his rifle and web gear. Checking the canteens, he finds that both are bone dry. Reluctantly, he opens his own canteen and holds it to the boy's lips. Mattison sucks greedily, and Andy has to pull hard on the canteen to get it away from him.

"Okay, Mattison," he says, "this hill is a motherfucker, but you can do it. Don't make us carry you."

"Jesus," Mattison says, "I can't get up. I can't."

But his feet are moving beneath him; his hands are pressing against the red earth. Somehow, he makes it to his feet. Relieved of his burdens, he is able to continue the upward climb. The column is moving again.

Mattison is not the only one who is hurting. The trail is littered with items of food, clothing and equipment jettisoned by the men to lighten their loads. Andy will not resort to this. He refuses to share his gear with Charlie.

Somehow, through a sheer effort of will, Third Platoon makes it to the top of Hill 237. They find some old foxholes there, but no signs of recent activity. Lieutenant Berry calls for a five-minute break, and the men sit down gratefully to rest. Biggs lights up a smoke and offers the pack to Andy. Even though he has been carrying Roddy Mattison's pack as well as his own, he has barely broken a sweat. At this moment, the last thing that Andy wants is a cigarette, and he waves off the pack. He hopes that Biggs cannot see how tired he is.

With trembling hands, Andy takes out his canteen, now barely half full, and unscrews the cap. Taking a careful sip, he sloshes the water around in his mouth, tantalizing his throat, which convulses in anticipation of its delicious wetness. Swallowing at last, he can feel it running all the way down his gullet. Raising the canteen to his lips again, he lets a little trickle down his throat, and a little more… and loses control. His hands gripping the canteen, his greedy mouth and throat, refuse to obey the instructions of his brain. In a matter of seconds, he has sucked down every last drop of his water.

Putting the canteen away, he looks around guiltily to see if anyone has noticed. It was a stupid cherry mistake, not something a squad leader should do. To make matters worse, his mouth feels as cottony as if he has had nothing to drink at all. At least he will no longer have to suffer the agony of temptation.

Dingle Berry gets Captain Roth on the horn. Andy cannot hear what is being said, but from the look on the lieutenant's face, he can tell that he is being given an ass chewing for being behind schedule. It comes as no surprise, therefore, when the word is given that they are moving out again.

It seems impossible, but going down the hill proves to be even harder than coming up. They are met with a wall of brush so thick, they cannot cut their way through it. The lieutenant sends scouts out to look for a trail, and a dry stream bed is located. Bushes growing alongside it spread their branches overhead, forming a tunnel, and it is necessary for the men to proceed downward on their hands and knees. In the stream bed the earth has been washed away, leaving a covering of stones that cut their hands and shred the cloth of their trousers. They are beasts, driven beyond the limits of their endurance, yet continuing dumbly on. Any thought of trying to trap Charlie is out the window. Their only concern is to get themselves off that terrible hill.

As he crawls along through a haze of suffering, every cell and fiber of Andy's body is crying out for water. Imagining the water rushing down that same course during the rainy season only a short time before nearly drives him mad. He is thoroughly pissed off, and with every exhalation of breath he repeats a mantra that calls for a reckoning, from whom or what he neither knows nor cares.

Payback… payback… payback….

It seems as if the torture will never end, and it comes as a pleasant surprise when the ground begins to level out and the vegetation at last thins enough to allow him to stand. Dazed, he stumbles with the others out of the woods at the edge of a rice paddy.

The paddy is flooded. Its water is swimming with parasites, amoebic dysentery and God knows what else. Andy does not care. It is wet. Crawling out onto a dike, he dips one of his empty canteens into the brown sludge.

"Cullen! What the hell do you think you're doing? Put that canteen away, that's an order! That goes for the rest of you men, too- anyone drinking paddy water will be looking at an Article 15."

Andy knows that in this case, Dingle Berry is right. He feels ashamed as he puts away his canteen. Christ, he is supposed to be setting an example.

Artie Sugg, the leader of the first squad, is peering back at the hill behind them with a strange look on his face.

"Sir," he says, "I hate to say this, and I hope to hell I'm wrong, but ain't that the same side of the hill where we started up this morning?"

Lieutenant Berry's jaw drops, and his eyes pop open wide. Taking out his compass, he points it in the direction of the hill. Shaking his head, he lets out a high-pitched giggle.

"Well I'll be damned," he says. "Sarge, I do believe you're right. We must have got turned around somehow when we were coming down."

"What 're we gonna do, lieutenant? We ain't got time to go over the hill again, and the men are all purty well whipped anyways."

"I'll tell what we're going to do," says the lieutenant. "We're going to do what we should have done in the first place. We're going to go around the sonofabitch. I won't tell anybody if you don't."

*

As they approach the village, Pothead Huggins steps in a foot trap. Andy hears him screaming and comes upon him sitting beside the trail with the nylon upper of his left boot soaked with blood. Although the steel plate in the insole protected the bottom of his foot when it went in, punji sticks embedded in the sides of the hole pointing downward caught his ankle when he tried to pull it out. Huggins will be rewarded for his stupidity with a Purple Heart and time off with round-eyed nurses.

Aside from the one minor incident, their trip into Binh Duc is uneventful. The ville has been secured by the other platoons of Alpha Company, and if there was any resistance, it has been suppressed. The men make a beeline for the well, where they drink until their stomachs are as round and hard as watermelons and have a happy time playing grabass and dousing one another with water, until their leaders manage to restore a semblance of order.

After drinking their fill, Andy and Willie Biggs wander over to the place where a group of villagers are waiting under the guard of a squad from First Platoon, old people and a few mothers with children. No officers are in evidence, but they find Billy Vo, the Vietnamese interpreter who travels with their battalion, in the process of interrogating a boy who looks to be about twelve years old. Billy knows Andy well, having worked with him before. When he sees Andy coming, he goes to meet him, grabbing the boy by the hair and propelling him along in front of him.

"This one hide in duck pond, Tah-git. Breathe through reed. Him know something, but him no talk. Maybe VC."

Andy studies the boy, a scruffy little kid wearing wet pajamas that are too big for him, with a narrow pockmarked face topped by an unruly thatch of jet-black hair. Although thin, he is wiry, a tough-looking little bastard. Perhaps he is older than he appears.

"You didn't have any luck with any of the others?"

"No, Tah-git. Others scared, say no VC. Him no scared. No say nothing, but him know something."

"Does he have any family here?"

Billy nods and points out a woman squatting next to a little girl.

"That woman boy's mothah. Gel sistah."

Andy turns to Willie Biggs.

"Take the sister behind that house over there and shoot her."

Biggs walks over to the mother and child grinning evilly, and takes the girl by the arm. The woman grabs her daughter's other arm, and a tug of war begins in which it looks as if the child may be torn apart. Andy goes to help Biggs, prying the woman's fingers loose. She grovels in the dirt, clinging to his legs and wailing, as Biggs leads the child out of sight behind the house. A few moments later, there comes a staccato burst from Biggs' M-16. The mother shrieks and crumples to the ground.

The color has drained from the boy's face, but he manages to maintain a defiant expression. Andy wonders if Biggs has really shot the child, or understood that he meant this merely as a ploy to get the boy to talk. It is merely idle curiosity on his part. It is hard for someone who thinks of himself as dead to have much concern for the living. He strolls over to the house and meets Biggs coming in the opposite direction. Behind the house, Peter Plumb is guarding the girl.

Billy rattles off a stream of angry Vietnamese, slapping the boy's face several times for emphasis. The boy glares back at him and remains silent.

Andy motions again to Biggs, who lifts the mother up and leads her, stumbling but unresisting, behind the house. The air is rent by a piercing scream. God knows what Biggs has done to the woman to induce it. The boy flinches, but is otherwise unmoved. A cool customer, and definitely VC, no doubt about it.

"Tell him my patience is used up," Andy says. "Tell him that if he doesn't give us something, I will kill him now."

Once more Billy spits a rapid fire stream of Vietnamese, and once more the boy holds fast. Andy feels a grudging admiration for the boy, but he will not let that prevent him from doing what he has to.

"All right, my friend," he tells him, "you asked for it."

Slowly, dramatically, so that the boy will have plenty of time to consider what is about to happen to him, Andy unsheathes his bayonet and fixes it to his rifle. He advances with a look of such sheer, murderous hatred that the boy cannot help but cringe. As Andy comes closer, the boy backs up until his retreat is blocked by the wall of a hut. Every eye in the village is on Andy, as he tickles the boy's throat with the bayonet. The boy's eyes are closed, his expression resigned. He is prepared to die. A collective gasp escapes the villagers, as the bayonet slices through the boy's shirt and lays it open. A thin line of red springs out on the exposed skin from throat to navel. The boy shudders and, opening his eyes, looks down at his stomach. Seeing what has been done to him, he jerks his head up and spits in Andy's face.

It is what Andy has been waiting for. With lightning speed, he whips his rifle around, clouting the boy on the jaw with a vertical butt stroke. As the boy falls, he kicks him viciously in the groin.

"Cullen! What the hell are you doing?"

Drawn by the sound of gunfire, Lieutenant Berry has come to investigate, and is horrified by what he sees.

"Stay out of this, LT. I'm interrogating this prisoner."

The lieutenant is regarding Andy with the wariness that a circus trainer might reserve for the tigers in his care. The boy lies doubled up, writhing in pain. Billy kneels beside him and speaks to him quietly, and the boy answers him through clenched teeth.

"Him no talk," says Billy apologetically.

"Back off, Cullen," says the lieutenant. "They'll interrogate him

157

back at G-2. Get on the horn and call for a chopper to come and pick him up. That's an order."

Well, how about that? Who'd 've thought Dingle Berry had the stones?

"You got it, LT."

The chopper is coming. The pilot has contacted Andy, and is looking for Alpha Company's location.

"Can you pop smoke, Three-Six Alpha? I'm having trouble seeing you guys on the ground."

Andy is standing under the overhang of the roof of one of the houses. Checking his harness suspenders, he finds that he is fresh out of smoke grenades. Without a moment's hesitation, he pulls Horvath's lighter from his pocket and strikes a flame which he holds to the thatch above his head. Within seconds, the roof is blazing, sending up billowing clouds of smoke. The hedge row catches fire as well, and the sound of the bamboo exploding is like rifle fire.

"I see white smoke," the pilot says.

"That's a rog," Target replies.

Printed in the United States
56321LVS00004B/65

9 780897 542197